CisLuna

Books by Ejner Fulsang

A Destiny of Fools

A Knavish Piece of Work

SpaceCorp

EJNER FULSANG

_____

CisLuna

For Aunt Ellen !

Enjoy !

Århus Publishing

Copyright

© Ejner Fulsang, 2017

Author's photograph by Philip Hutcherson

Nathalie Cabrol's photograph by Deborah Kolyer of SETI

Other Scientist and Project Manager photographs in Acknowledgements section are courtesy of NASA

Cover art by Douglas Shrock www.shrox.com

SAN: 850–3052

ISBN (Amazon Kindle eBook): 978-0-9913243-7-8

ISBN (Createspace Paperback): 978-0-9913243-8-5

For Julie, the woman who changed my life

TABLE OF CONTENTS

Foreword—NASA Scientist Brian Day

There is a fascinatingly anachronistic quality to CisLuna. It reads like a classic hard-boiled detective novel from the early to mid-20th century. Much of the banter between characters takes the reader back to those bygone days. There is certainly more than a little of Sam Spade in Roy Stone. But the setting, in dramatic contrast, is distinctly futuristic. In the background remains the image of the dystopian Earth described in SpaceCorp, the prequel to this novel. The region of Low Earth Orbit has been rendered unusable due to the Kessler Effect. But the central setting for this story is the Moon and the area around it, cislunar space.

True to form, Ejner Fulsang has been painstaking in doing his research. He describes in exquisite detail the technologies and methodologies that will be used to live and work on and near the Moon. This technical part of the story is in remarkable accord with the kinds of discussions you will hear today at conferences around the world as the space agencies of many nations as well as a growing number of private companies come together to plan a vigorous renewed effort to explore and establish a sustained presence on the Moon.

Why all of the interest in the Moon? Why would it merit such a significant role in this story? Why is there now such a clamor among governments and industry to get there? Such was certainly not the case even relatively recently. In the years following the premature termination of the Apollo program, the lunar science and exploration communities dwindled to a small fraction of their former numbers. The Moon seemed so less interesting than other worlds, whose wonders were being revealed by robotic probes venturing into deep space. As a kid growing up during the space race, I learned in school that the Moon was geologically dead, completely airless, and utterly dry. So much of what we learned about the Moon back then turned out to be completely wrong!

Reexamining old Apollo seismometer data, a team led by lunar scientist Clive Neal of Notre Dame came to the remarkable conclusion that the Moon is seismically active, experiencing moonquakes measuring greater than 5.5 on the Richter scale, sometimes lasting for more than 10 minutes. Be assured right here and now, that if you were to experience a quake of that magnitude and duration, you would very quickly conclude that the object you were standing on was not geologically dead!

During the time interval of 2010 - 2014, I had the good fortune to work with the brilliant scientists and engineers of NASA's Lunar Atmosphere and Dust Environment Explorer (LADEE) mission. In 2013, this robotic explorer entered into lunar orbit, then dropped down low to fly through the Moon's atmosphere, studying its structure, composition, and variability over time. The Moon does indeed have an atmosphere, technically a surface boundary exosphere. This extremely tenuous assemblage of gasses is an example of what is likely the most common type of atmosphere in our solar system. Mercury has one. The Moon has one. Larger asteroids and many moons of the giant planets have them. Even some larger members of the Kuiper Belt; distant, small, icy worlds beyond the orbit of Neptune have them. The Moon provided us with an opportunity to study an example of this extreme type of atmosphere from a location right in our own back yard, astronomically speaking.

Prior to LADEE, I spent several years assigned to a particularly exciting mission, the Lunar CRater Observation and Sensing Satellite - LCROSS. In 2009, this NASA mission used the Centaur upper stage of its Atlas V rocket as a high-speed impactor directed into a permanently-shadowed region in the crater Cabeus near the Moon's south pole. The impact excavated hundreds of tons of material from the crater floor, sending it up, out of the shadows, into the sunlight, and high into the sky of the Moon. The robotic LCROSS spacecraft then dove down into this plume, analyzing its composition and confirming the presence of significant amounts water ice and other volatiles that had been sequestered in the shadows. Subsequent studies using the Lunar Reconnaissance Orbiter (LRO), revealed that the deposits of polar water ice on the Moon may amount to billions of tons. So much for a waterless Moon!

This changed everything. Habitation of the Moon and its environs became much more feasible with large amounts of this precious resource at hand. There could now be ample water to drink and oxygen to breathe. Freed from the complications of having to traverse the Earth's thick atmosphere and deep gravity well, the Moon will offer a great, economical alternative to the Earth as a source for delivery of oxygen and hydrogen fuel to orbiting spacecraft preparing to venture to far more distant locations. The Moon will become a critical stepping stone as we spread out across the solar system. This earns the Moon its prominent role in plans for space exploration. And it makes it a very appropriate setting for Ejner's story.

A truly amazing community is working together right now to advance our understanding of the Moon, our solar system, and now even other solar systems, and turn our dreams of becoming a spacefaring society into reality. It is fitting that

Ejner recognizes some of them in this story through the naming of spacecraft and stations such as the Anthony Colaprete, John Marmie, Nathalie Cabrol, and William Borucki. These people, and so many other pioneers of space today comprise a real-life cast of characters every bit as fascinating and colorful as you could find in a Fulsang novel.

But the adventure of the Moon does not just belong to this group of scientists and engineers. It belongs to all of us, students, backyard astronomers, and anyone with that all-important spark of curiosity. During the LCROSS mission, K-12 students around the world took remote control from their classrooms of some of the giant radio dishes of the Goldstone Station of the Deep Space Network to help monitor the health and status of the LCROSS spacecraft in flight through the GAVRT program (http://www.lewiscenter.org/gavrt/). Amateur astronomers regularly observe and record meteoroid impact flashes on the Moon (http://alpo-astronomy.org/lunarupload/lunimpacts.htm); an activity that became particularly scientifically important during the LADEE mission as we studied meteoroid impacts as one of the sources for the lunar atmosphere. Citizen scientists can identify and map interesting features on the Moon at home using Moon Mappers (https://cosmoquest.org/x/science/moon/). Web applications like NASA's Moon Trek (https://moontrek.jpl.nasa.gov/) allow the public to explore the Moon in dramatic detail, and view it through the eyes of many different instruments aboard many different spacecraft. One night every year, people gather in hundreds of coordinated events around the world to participate in International Observe the Moon Night (http://observethemoonnight.org/).

The Moon beckons irresistibly with its promise for the future. It is more accessible than ever before with tools and activities available to people of all ages and backgrounds. Join us in the great adventure of exploring the Moon! And while you are at it, sit back and enjoy a good read about exploration and mystery on and around the Moon, as depicted in CisLuna.

—Brian Day
2017

Mauna Kea, Hawaii – 4207 meters
Subaru and Keck I and II Telescopes in the background

Brian Day is the Lead for Lunar and Planetary Mapping and Modeling, as well as Lead for Citizen Science and Outreach at NASA's Solar System Exploration Research Virtual Institute (SSERVI). As project manager for Lunar and Planetary Mapping and Modeling, he oversees development of data visualization and analysis tools designed for mission planning, planetary science, education, and public outreach. In his citizen science role, he coordinates programs providing opportunities for students and the public to directly participate in NASA science and exploration. From 2010-2014, Brian served as the Education/Public Outreach Lead for NASA's Lunar Atmosphere and Dust Environment Explorer (LADEE) mission to the Moon, which flew through and studied the Moon's tenuous atmosphere. From 2007-2010 he served as the E/PO Lead for NASA's LCROSS lunar impactor mission which discovered deposits of water ice at the Moon's South Pole. Brian has participated in various NASA Mars Analog Field Studies, supporting scientific research and robotic rover tests in extreme environments here on Earth. In 2007, he flew on the Aurigid-MAC mission to record fragments of comet Kiess entering Earth's upper atmosphere. As a member of NASA's Speakers Bureau, he is sent by NASA to give talks on a wide range of NASA missions and research topics.

PROLOGUE

Key events of 2028 to 2085:

2028—Kessler Syndrome renders Low Earth Orbit, or LEO, non-viable for conventional satellites.

2030—SpaceCorp initiates construction of the SpaceCorp Space Station *SSS Wernher Von Braun*, a one kilometer spinning ring advertised as the first debris-proof instrument-hosting space station.

2038—The *Von Braun* is christened. 45 astronauts are killed and 427 wounded by debris strikes during its eight-year construction.

2070—Sea level rise: +5 meters since 2010; atmospheric CO_2 at 800 parts per million

2073—Dissolution of America

January 1st, 2073—Dixieland repeals Emancipation Proclamation, 210 years after President Lincoln issued it.

August 4th, 2073—Promised Land passes legislation providing tax incentives for polygamous families. Three days later a rider is attached stipulating that the tax incentives only apply to families involving one husband and multiple wives.

2074—SpaceCorp initiates exodus to CisLuna; *SSS Albert Einstein* is first space station to take up residence at the Earth-Moon L1 Lagrange point. It is followed a year later by *SCS Pelican*.

2084—Sierra, sovereign state of SpaceCorp, hires mercenaries to seal the border along the Colorado River to protect against land hungry Mormon pioneers from Promised Land.

PART I

CHAPTER ONE

August 2085

Some people need to remind themselves that they'd been something once. Police Chief Carmine Ciccolella was like that. He had dozens of cardboard boxes along his office walls—old hardcopy case files that he wasn't ready to say goodbye to.

"Hiya, Chick, what's up?"

The Chief looked up from his monitor but didn't smile. "Sit down, Roy. Close the door."

I sat down and mopped the sweat off my face with my bandana. His office had an air conditioner mounted in the window and the breeze felt good. It.was some old junker he'd restored with parts from the scrap yards around Lompoc. SpaceCorp could be counted upon for three hots and a cot, but your personal comfort depended on your ability to scrounge things—old things, discarded things, things people didn't want anymore. Scroungers were king around here.

"Remember how I asked if I could tap you for a homicide if the need arose?"

"Yeah, *I* remember. I was hoping *you* didn't."

"'Sorry, Roy. I need to call in that marker."

I used to be a CID agent back when I was in the Army before the Dissolution. I did homicide back then. Was pretty good at it too until one of my cases went sideways. Because of that I had an agreement with the Chief that I would stick with property crimes unless he was in a jam.

"Smitty and Anderson can't handle it?" I asked.

"Smitty and Anderson each have two cases already, and I got the mayor of V-berg crawling up my ass to close 'em."

"Two cases? That's not that big a stretch, Chief."

"It is if the third case is in CisLuna."

"We had a murder in space?"

"We've got a dozen stations orbiting around Earth-Moon L1, a space port construction yard at L2, and three water works on the lunar surface. Altogether that's over fifteen thousand people counting transients. It had to happen sooner or later."

"Okay, so where did this one happen?"

"*SSS Albert Einstein*, a research vessel up in EML1. The captain is whining about crew morale. Here's the case file."

He handed me a stick. I put it in the reader port on my communicator.

"There's nothing on it."

"Yeah, I need you to fix that. You're gonna be lead investigator. We're scrambling a personal lunar direct shuttle just for you." He looked at his monitor, "*SLS John Marmie*. It's gonna take you straight to *Einstein*. There's a chopper outside waiting to take you to Edwards. You're gonna launch as soon as you get there and get suited up."

"Suited up?"

"Yeah, it's a Low Earth Orbit shuttle and since LEO shuttles don't usually go to the Moon, they're not pressurized."

"You're gonna make me late for dinner."

The chopper was an old Army Blackhawk, kept flying more by miracles than maintenance. They flew with the cargo doors open because of the heat. It was 40°C at V-berg and Edwards was supposed to top 50°C. The crew chief fixed me up with a helmet and showed me how to plug in my communicator so I could call my wife.

"What's that noise? I can hardly hear you!" Emily said.

"I'm being sent on assignment to space."

"Oh my god! Where in space?"

"A station out in CisLuna. On *Albert Einstein*. There's been a murder."

"Why'd they pick you?" Emily asked.

"The regular homicide guys are busy and I have a homicide background."

Even with the chopper noise drowning her out, I could tell she was not happy.

"I thought you were going to stick with property crimes."

"Yeah, well, something came up."

"I'm worried."

"What, about me going to space?"

"You know what I mean."

"I know. Look, this perp is 370 thousand klicks away. You'll be safe down here on Earth."

Silence.

"Maybe you should take Devil and go stay with Becky," I said. Devil was our German shepherd. He was a big brute, forty-five kilos, jet black with white stockings.

"I was gonna make steaks tonight. I got some nice filets."

"Real beef?"

"The butcher said they were."

"Can you freeze them?"

"I think I'll cook them. Devil's gonna get yours."

Dial tone.

I hoped she'd see reason and take the steaks and Devil and camp out at Becky's for a while.

CHAPTER TWO

Edwards Air Field used to be Edwards Air Force Base until SpaceCorp bought it. The Rogers Dry Lake runway system was perfect for space launches using big Air Launch Vehicles or ALVs with their LEO shuttles slung under their wings. Big as battleships. If an ALV crashed on a return flight, you just bulldoze the wreckage into the Mojave and carry on. Fortunately, that never happened with an ALV although we have lost a few LEO shuttles from debris impacts up in space.

For fifty years space debris, aka the Kessler Effect, made LEO non-navigable for satellites. SpaceCorp solved that problem with its fleet of giant manned space stations. They were big rotating spoked wheels, a kilometer in diameter and heavily armored for debris resistance. Satellite instruments were mounted out of harm's way along the interior spokes. Still, occasional damage did occur from time to time, hence the need for human crews to keep up with repairs. But that left the problem of getting crews up to the stations.

Cheap was the name of the game when you needed to get millions of tons of cargo into LEO, and the ALV-LEO shuttle combination could loft a hundred tonnes of cargo or people into orbit for the cost of the fuel.

My welcoming committee rushed me from the helicopter into the passenger prep terminal in a golf cart. I was glad for the open-air ride. It was wicked hot on the tarmac. Inside the terminal I stripped down to my pubes and put my street clothes into a small duffle bag that I would carry onboard. A trained astronaut can suit up solo, but since I was a rube, it took two flight techs to dress me. And dress me they did, one layer at a time, starting with my nappy which the techs assured me would collect six hour's worth of piss in a manner I was not supposed to notice on the flight to CisLuna. My space suit was roughly my size. It had lacings that could be tightened to make the legs shorter and lacings that could be loosened to make the arms longer—handy when you're built like a gorilla.

One of the techs was obviously proud of his product—like he'd designed it himself. He babbled on about how SpaceCorp space suits were way more advanced versions of NASA's old Constellation Space Suit.

"Full pressure," he said. "No need to breathe pure oxygen for two hours before going into space. Did I mention this suit comes in two configurations?"

"No."

"You're in a Config One. It's used for travel to and from Earth plus limited EVAs in the event of an emergency. It's optimized for comfort and agility within the space shuttle. Life support is only good for about two hours."

"What am I supposed to do for the other four hours?"

"Umbilicals. I'll hook you up when you get inside the shuttle. Your suit is pressurized to 0.8 atmospheres—same as modern airliners. That's so you don't have to hyperventilate on pure O2 for two hours before flight. It also has a backpack parachute and a life raft in the event of a shuttle breakup or ditch."

I was sorry I asked, but hey, in for a penny! "What's a Config Two?"

"Extended EVAs."

"EVAs?"

"Extra Vehicular Activity. It's optimized for ballistic protection from microjunk—there's still quite a lot of it up there. It also has an Extravehicular Mobility Unit, or EMU, that weighs 136 kg. All that comes in a special back pack that also has a propulsion unit for scooting around independent of your tether. Without the EMU, Config Two suits can be used for work on the lunar surface. They have life support for 150 hours, subject to the intensity of the work being performed."

I guess the reality that I was going into space was beginning to sink in because suddenly I started asking a zillion stupid questions.

"How long is the flight?"

"About six hours from drop-off to docking at *Einstein*."

"I've gotta stay in a suit the whole way? Why isn't this crate pressurized?"

"Low Earth Orbit is full of space debris. If you get a hull penetration, it just passes out the other side. There's no depressurization emergency because everyone is already in their suit."

"What if that piece of debris passes through me?"

"Your ticket will be refunded to your next of kin."

"I didn't pay anything for it."

"Then your next of kin won't get very much."

"How do I pee?"

"I already told you, just pee. You're wearing that special diaper and won't feel the wetness. Keep this bag with you. In addition to your personal effects, it has a small supply of replacement diapers, plus some special wipes to clean your nether parts when you get a chance to change back into street clothes."

"Where's my gun?"

"The weapons clerk took it—no firearms in space. SpaceCorp policy. You can retrieve it when you get back."

"How do I take a shit?"

"Same as peeing. But you'll feel the fecal matter until you get your suit off and change your diaper."

"What if I get thirsty?"

"You have two straws you can suck on. One is plain water. The other is laced with nutrients and electrolytes—your 'inflight meal.'"

"Can I open the visor to scratch my nose?"

"Sure. ONCE!"

After I got suited, the techs piled me back on the golf cart and drove me out to the colossal air launch vehicle. Did I say it was big as a battleship? Make that an aircraft carrier. Add to that a LEO shuttle the size of a destroyer hanging under the midpoint of the wing. Maybe being up close is making me exaggerate, but not by much though. I noticed the ALV had no fuselage.

"Where does the crew sit in that thing?" I asked.

"They don't. It's fully autonomous."

"No humans at all?"

"That's to avoid exposing them to gamma radiation from the shuttle engines when they ignite at the drop-off point."

"Drop-off point?"

"Yes, several hundred kilometers over the ocean and about twenty kilometers up. The shuttle gets released, and its engines ignite after it falls a few hundred meters. The shuttle and ALV need a proper safety clearance. Then the ALV turns around and comes back home to Edwards."

"So then what?"

"So then you keep flying to CisLuna."

"Isn't there a bunch of radiation out there?"

"You mean the Van Allen belts? Not to worry. Think of them as giant concentric doughnuts circling the Earth. Instead of flying through them on the way to the Moon, your shuttle will just hop over them."

Underneath the shuttle was an escalator that led up through an open belly hatch. I lost one of my flight technicians here and the remaining one escorted me up into the hull.

"Those big drop tanks you saw suspended from the wings?"

"Yeah?"

"Those are liquid hydrogen or LH2 as we call it. That's the propellant used by the nuclear lightbulbs to make thrust."

"How much thrust?"

"Five million Newtons each—enough to accelerate you at about one gee. You'll make thrust for about twenty minutes to get up to full speed. Then you'll feel MECO, main engine cut off. At that point, you'll just glide to CisLuna. When you get close to your destination the engines will use the internal LH2 tank to decelerate. We call it a flip-and-burn maneuver. Okay, here's your seat."

He strapped me in, then explained how to unstrap if things went sideways. "This is your O2 umbilical. You'll want to use that to conserve the O2 in your suit tank. Make sure this needle stays in the green zone."

"What do I do if it goes out of green?"

"Switch to your suit tank and ask for assistance. The suit tank is only good for about two hours.

"This is your water line. It's for cooling you down if you get too hot. You have a water bottle attached to your suit but you'll want to save that."

He checked me out and then said, "Okay, now I'm going to activate your HUD and get you connected to the onboard wifi."

A HUD display popped up about a third of a meter in front of my helmet visor.

"You can select different viewing perspectives outside the shuttle using this panel on your forearm." He showed me a flap that was secured with hook and loop tape. "Okay, I have to go now. Safe flight!"

It took an hour to reach the drop-off point, 20 klicks up and another 250 klicks out over the Pacific Ocean. While we were climbing, a passenger named Patty showed me how to set my intercom so we could have a private conversation.

"That way we won't interfere with the crew," she said. "I'm hitching a ride on this shuttle so I can get back to CisLuna faster."

I looked around the cabin. She and I were the only seats occupied out of what looked like thirty seats.

"Couldn't they squeeze in a few more hitchhikers? Seems a waste, just the two of us."

"They could've, but this was a short notice flight. I got lucky because I was in the hangar and they needed somebody to babysit a newbie. Normally, I'd have to catch a ride to a LEO station. Then a day or so later, I'd grab a cislunar shuttle for a run to one of the stations in CisLuna. If that happens to be the station I want, I'm in luck. If not, I'd have to wait for a shuttle going to the station I *do* want. It can take a week of shuttling around."

"What if you want to go to the Moon?" I asked.

"Then I'd have to go to *SSS William Borucki*—that's the only station that services the lunar colonies. Add another week to the trip."

"So why do we rate special treatment?"

"You tell me. You're the VIP on this flight."

She looked at me waiting for an answer. I didn't say anything.

A bit later I felt my stomach trying to crawl up my throat. I looked at Patty.

"Drop-off," she said.

My nausea dissipated when the engines ignited a moment later. Acceleration at 1-gee felt like being strapped onto one of those form-fitting thermal mattresses with lots of clothes on. It lasted maybe twenty minutes. At MECO the weightless sensation returned.

"Are you nauseous?" she asked.

"No. Not exactly. Maybe a little... yeah."

Patty got out of her seat and floated over to my side. She undid the flap on my arm panel and hit a switch. A straw popped up inside my helmet.

"Sip on this. It's strong. Two sips will relax your stomach. Anything more and you go to sleep. No more than four sips! If your vitals start to fall off, the suit will start poking you with needles to counteract the joy juice. Got that? Four sips, no more."

"Okay."

I awakened to Patty knocking on my helmet.

"Rise and shine, Roy-Boy! We're docking with *Einstein*, and you don't want to be carried off. It marks you as a chako."

"What's a chako?"

"Short for chechako, a rube. First trip to space."

"Thanks. Wouldn't want that."

"Flip your HUD over to Channel 6 and you can get a pilot's eye view of our approach."

I did. "Jesus, is that thing as big as it looks?"

"Yup. *Einstein* is a one klick in diameter. It rotates at 1.34 rpm for a full gee of artificial gravity at the outer rim. The shuttle's onboard computer has to match our approach speed with the station's 70-meter per second rim speed. Once we attach, we get pulled into the ring like one of those elevators on an aircraft carrier. You'll be feeling like you're strapped in upside down. Watch what I do to get out of your seat without falling on your head. For now, just sit tight until they open the belly hatch. I'll lead you over to the airlock that takes you to the passenger area—it's fully pressurized. The space station is also kept at a full atmosphere. You'll be able to get out of that suit once you get in the visitor's suit locker area. Did you wet your nappies?"

"I can't tell, but I do have to piss like a racehorse."

"Try to hold it. You should be out of that suit in another twenty minutes. I hope you're not shy. Everything is pretty much co-ed up here."

Patty released her quick disconnect straps and rotated onto the shuttle ceiling by holding onto a trapeze bar that flipped down in front of her seat. The shuttle ceiling had a built-in walkway with hand holds. Before she departed, she made sure I got out of my seat without breaking my neck. It's a tricky maneuver, sort of like doing a loop-de-loop on the uneven bars. Once we were both on the 'ceiling,' we headed over to an escalator that thrust up through the belly hatch.

"What do you do up here, Patty?"

"I'm a shuttle jockey. I pilot personnel and cargo shuttles to the space stations up here in CisLuna—there are twelve of them."

"Thanks for babysitting me, Patty. I owe you."

"We're not quite done. I still have to get you through the airlock and into the passenger terminal. A flight tech will take over there."

It seemed weird to be stepping off the escalator and onto the shuttle's belly. It seemed weirder still to see the shuttle suspended upside down by her landing gear. She was a big son-of-a-bitch, a hundred meters long. The fuel they must have used to get me up here on short notice... somebody must want this case solved and fast.

After going through the airlock, I was greeted by another flight tech.

"Hi, Detective Stone. I'm Kevin. I'll be helping you get settled in on *Einstein*."

"Call me Roy."

"Okay, Roy, let's get you peeled down to your comfort liner. I imagine you'll want to use the head, sponge off a bit."

I looked around. Patty was across the room standing near a locker. More practiced by far with the debarking routine, she'd been quick to get out of her suit. She was buck naked except for an athletic looking bra holding her ample breasts. She had one foot on a bench and one hand holding her cheeks apart while she vigorously swabbed her nether parts. When she finished, she tossed the towelettes into a trash can that had a lid on it. She caught my eye. I blushed. She stuck out her tongue in a lewd smile and wiggled her buns at me.

Kevin caught my eye, "We're co-ed up here."

"So I've been told."

"Lowers the logistical burden not having to have separate facilities for the sexes."

"Makes sense."

"You'll get used to it."

I looked back at Patty. "I doubt that."

Kevin dragged me over to a row of lockers. "Here's your suit locker. I'm taping your name on it. Remember where it is! If there's an abandon station emergency, this is your top priority—get here and get your suit on. Then head for your escape pod."

I saw Patty, fully clothed, heading toward the door, her suit in a cart.

"She doesn't have a locker here?"

"She's a pilot. She'll stow her suit over by the shuttle craft. She just wanted to clean up a bit first."

"Oh."

There was an esoteric routine up here. Somehow I had to fit in.

"As soon as you're back in your street clothes, I'll take you to the... the victim's room. I'm told she's still there undisturbed."

"It's a woman?"

"Yes."

Fuck, it *would* have to be a woman.

CHAPTER THREE

Stiffs always have two things in common. They're dead and they stink. Even so, this one was peculiar. For one thing, she was hanging by her feet from the ceiling, her arms dangling down to the floor. For another she was completely nude.

I nodded to a tall dark-haired woman standing by the hatchway. At least she had on bunny slippers and gloves.

"You forensics?" I asked.

"Molecular biology."

Attractive, looks maybe forty, but really fit, almost muscle-bound. Probably make her closer to fifty actual. She held her left hand up casually revealing the outline of a wedding band under her rubber glove. *Mind reader too.*

"Have you examined the body?" I asked.

"They said wait for homicide."

"How long's that been?"

"They found her this morning when she missed shift change. She had the 4-8 watch. That was 16 hours ago. I got the call an hour after that."

"You think it happened between watches?"

"Yeah, somewhere between twenty hundred and oh four hundred."

"That's only twenty hours tops. What is it in here, five Celsius? She smells too much for the room to be that cold."

"I had them turn the temperature down as soon as I got here. It was thirty-five C when I showed up."

"Any chance it could have been longer than twenty hours?"

"She supposedly clocked out at twenty hundred last night."

"Supposedly?"

"We don't have any imagery from her work area. Just the usual entries consistent with her job function."

"Why no imagery?"

"Well, now that's a good question. Uh, should I call you Inspector or Detective?"

"Call me Roy, Roy Stone. I'm a detective. Brits are inspectors."

"I'm Monica Carvalho."

I started and jerked my head back toward her. "*The* Monica Carvalho?"

"Yes, *the* Monica Carvalho."

"What should I call *you*?"

"Monica's fine."

"Okay, pardon my asking, but why would they put somebody like you on this? Surely you got another doctor around here."

"She *was* the doctor. Well, one of them anyway."

"You knew her?"

"She delivered my last two kids."

"You two close?"

"Not really."

"Elaborate, please?"

"She was a good doctor. Too blond. Too ponytail. Too perky. It wore thin."

I looked at the upside-down doctor. She had the ponytail and she was definitely blond. The perky I'd have to leave to my imagination.

"You gonna be able to handle this? Autopsy and all?"

"No."

"Well, I'm gonna need an autopsy."

"There's a thousand people on this station. We have... or had four flight surgeons. One is seeing patients. The other two are between shifts."

I put on my bunnies and gloves and moved into the room. It was neat. Like the maid had just been there. Nothing knocked over, nothing out of place. I circled the body, not touching it. No wounds I could see. But her hair. Same shade as Hanna. A little younger maybe. Hard to tell upside-down. I shook my head and took a deep breath.

Monica stood in the hatchway. "You okay?" she asked.

"Yeah." I took my kerchief out of my hip pocket and mopped my brow.

"Is this your first murder?"

"No."

"I don't mean to pry but you look pretty shook up."

"I'm fine," I lied. "It's just... never mind. How long has she been here?"

"You already covered that. Maybe twenty hours."

"Oh, yeah. Upside down the whole time?"

"We decided not to move her until you had a look at her."

"There should be visible postmortem clotting in her arms and face. But there's nothing. She's pale as a ghost."

"So?"

"In a dead body, blood pools according to gravity and then clots. The clots show up as bruises. This woman has no visible bruising." I held up her hand to show Monica. "She doesn't even show any surface vascular definition."

Yes, this stiff was peculiar. They usually come with blood, or at least some of it. This one didn't have *any*.

We commandeered an operating room in sick bay for the autopsy. Flight Surgeon Tom Martin had volunteered for the honors. He spoke into a microphone at the end of a gooseneck that hung from the ceiling. Primitive, now that I think about it. I'd heard this station was old, launched up to CisLuna from LEO back in 2074. Monica stood at the victim's head assisting. I wandered around bugging everyone with my usual dumb questions.

"Victim's Name: Jessica Maloney. Caucasian female. Age 35. 173 cm. Weight 50 kg. Hmm... 4.5 kg less than her last physical, four months ago." He mopped his brow with a towel and tossed it onto the stainless steel table at his side. "That would be consistent with a complete loss of blood, Mr. Stone."

The doc picked up a scalpel, poised it over the victim, then put it down to mop his brow again.

"Did you know her?" I asked.

"She was a colleague."

"Not a friend?"

"Different shifts. Our paths didn't cross much. I knew her from reviewing her medical notes mostly." He took a deep breath. "But to your point, yes, I did know her."

"You want I should send for a coroner, say, from another station?"

"No!"

He seemed apologetic for raising his voice.

"I'll do whatever it takes to apprehend her killer," he said, his voice now resolute.

"Think that's the cause of death?" I asked, changing the subject. "She just bled out?"

"Maybe. Her body displays no sign of a struggle. She may have been heavily sedated while she was being drained. Or she may have already been dead."

"And by draining her blood, the murderer drained a lot of evidence with it," I said.

"Whoops, puncture wounds." Monica rolled the victim's head to the right and pointed at them with her index finger.

Martin bent to get a better look. "Two of them about 3 cm apart. They're very faint. Just above the clavicle along the common carotid artery."

"Why two in the same artery?" I asked.

"Maybe the murderer missed with the first one?" Monica asked.

"One way to find out," Martin said. He began a shallow incision along the neck. A moment later the carotid artery was exposed, showing two clear puncture wounds.

"Could the first jab have gone all the way through? Made the perp think he missed?" I asked.

Martin stuck a gloved finger under the artery and pulled it out exposing the underside. "Doesn't appear so."

"Check the top of her head," I said. "If he drained her from the neck only, there should be bruising at the top of her head."

Monica canted the victim's head up and parted the hair.

"No bruising," she said. But I've got several more puncture wounds."

Dr. Martin leaned over to examine the site.

"The carotid artery extends over the top of the skull. The bastard seems to have more than a passing competency with human anatomy," Monica said.

"Yes," Martin said. "This was not just some casual phlebotomist. They only tap veins. Tapping an artery requires the skills of a doctor."

Monica turned the victim's head further to the side exposing the back of the neck and a faint crescent of indentations.

"Are those teeth marks?" I asked.

"Gentlemen, we appear to have a vampire in our midst," Monica said.

CHAPTER FOUR

"There a place a guy can get a drink around here?" I asked Monica. It had been a long day. "I just need to spin down a bit before I turn in."

"Albert's. It's not much but it's close by."

Albert's turned out to be a bit more than 'not much.' The ceiling was made of tiled monitors that combined their images to show the Moon spinning in real time. Pretty cool. You could make out all the craters. The rest of the bar had some kind of faux-wood paneling and faux-wood flooring. I'd figured out that 'faux-wood' was the local euphemism for nanocellulose. Everything on this crate was made out of nanocellulose—tensile strength of aluminum, stiff as Kevlar®, and strength-to-weight eight times better than stainless steel. *Einstein* had been overbuilt in LEO to withstand the constant impact of space junk, and now she depended on that same armor to shield her crew from the ten-rem annual radiation levels of cislunar space. She was Logan 'Mack' MacGregor's brainchild. Mack was as close to royalty as you could get in SpaceCorp and I was sitting across a faux-wood table enjoying a nightcap with his lovely wife.

I ordered a Scotch and Monica got an Armagnac—Albert's was nothing if not well-stocked. Neither of us said anything while we waited for the drinks. I looked at the ceiling display so I wouldn't have to make conversation. After the waiter put them on the table, I tried to pay only to discover that like everything else in SpaceCorp, booze was free, subject to rationing, of course. We clinked our glasses and each took a sip. I was having a hard time not staring at her. She cast her eyes down at her drink and shifted in her seat. I thought she was going to get up and leave, but she didn't.

"You flashed your wedding band at me earlier."

"Did I?"

"'Sorry. I wasn't checking you out. It's what I do when I go into crime-scene-investigator mode. All on or all off."

She said nothing, just gave me a half smile.

"So where's your husband?"

"He's down on the surface."

"The Moon?"

"Earth. He commutes a lot."

More silence.

"What do you do up here when you're not crime-fighting?" I asked.

That got a smile.

"I'm trying to turn my rodent lab into a primate lab."

"Rats transmogrified into monkeys?"

That got a laugh.

"No, I've spent the last ten years genetically modifying rats so they'd be resistant to the 70-odd rems of radiation they'd encounter on a trip to the stars."

"You're gonna send rad-hard rodents to the stars! How're you gonna pull that off?"

She looked at me warily. "You know much about DNA?"

I nodded. "Got a working knowledge of it from forensics... we rely on it a lot for identification."

"So you know all DNA is equally prone to damage from radiation?"

"I do now."

"And as far as we know, all organisms are capable of repairing that damage, it's just that some are way better at it than others."

"Okay, I didn't know that either."

"The keys to our research are two micro-organisms, *Deinococcus radiodurans* and *Thermococcus gammatolerans*, that are better than all others at rapid DNA repair. Are you sure this conversation is spinning you down?"

"Actually, it is." I held up our two glasses up to signal the bartender for a refill. "It's completely taking my mind off the dead woman."

"Okay," she went on. "By isolating the genetic repair mechanisms of those two organisms and splicing it into the human genome and somehow getting it to express itself, we should eventually be able to engineer a rad-hard human. Just like we did with our rats."

"Whoa! Did you say rad-hard *human*? You're doing this on people?"

"Not initially. I've got three pairs of *Pan troglodytes* due here in a month."

"Pan what?"

"*Pan troglodytes*. They're the common chimp you see in zoos. We're going to use the lessons learned on rats to turn their offspring into a radiation resistant versions of their parents. They'll be a new species, *Pan astra*, stellar chimps."

"And then you're going to do the same thing to people. Everybody up here is going to be rad-hard?"

"Hell no! Backfilling all the DNA in all the cells of your body with the radiation repair gene is too much of a stretch. We'll select certain couples who want their children to be voyageurs. We'll modify the DNA in their fertilized eggs."

"So these future space farers will be born of normal humans?"

"Initially. Later they'll procreate with themselves. They'll be a new species. *Homo galacticus*. Unable to breed with humans ever again. They'll be galacticans."

"Born that way."

"Yes."

"What if they don't want to go to the stars?"

"They won't be forced to. We'll have lots to pick from."

"How so?"

"We're building a new class of space station designed for permanent positioning in the Main Belt Asteroids. In time, these new stations will become completely self-sufficient. Initially, they'll be located here at CisLuna. As we fill them up with galacticans, they'll move to the Belt."

This was bugging me. "But what if they don't want to move to the Belt?"

"As I said, they won't have to. They could stay here at CisLuna where they're born. Or they could even go to Earth and live among humans."

"Won't they be ostracized?"

"You won't be able to tell them from regular people. They'll just be shorter by 20 or 25 centimeters. Perfectly proportioned. We'll be using genes from Pygmies to constrain their height. We're not inducing dwarfism."

I looked around the bar. We were alone except for the bartender washing glasses. "I keep thinking you're going to bust out laughing and yell, 'April Fools!'"

She didn't even smile. "It's no joke. We're doing this. It's gonna happen."

I leaned across the table and stared hard at her. "A new species of human. A *galactican*?"

"Yup."

"Well, I can see why you're doing it up here. Earthside,

you'd be burned at the stake by the religious right, not to mention the anti-eugenics types."

"Yup."

"But why a new species? Aren't there advances in shielding? I gotta say this *sounds* like eugenics."

"It's not eugenics. It's a necessity for survival. Where we're sitting right now, the ambient external radiation is about 10 rems per year. We can and do shield for that, so you're safe here so long as you stay inside. However, we have to keep a close eye on shuttle pilots like Patty. If she rems out and can't find a new indoor job to transition into, she will be Earthbound. A groundie.

"Interplanetary space is about 25 rems ambient. Worse if you venture close to the gas giants—they'll fry you in an instant. We could shield for 25 rems but we'd take a huge mass hit in the process. You know about mass fractions?"

"Not a thing."

"Wet mass over dry mass. A typical interplanetary ship would come in around eighteen. That means if you add a kilogram of dry mass—structure, shielding, food, people—you have to add eighteen kilos of propellant.

"We're planning to have permanent colonies in the Main Belt Asteroids—galacticans who are born there, live their lives there, and die there. Asteroids will be critical for stores replenishment when we arrive at distant stars, far more important than so-called habitable planets. It's a lot easier to lasso an ore-rich asteroid than descend into a planet's gravity well, hunt for ore deposits, dig or excavate for that ore, refine it, and haul it back up to an orbiting space station or star ship.

"But the biggest argument for *Homo galacticus* is interstellar space where the ambient radiation is 70 rems per year. *Homo sapiens* wouldn't survive. And shielding for a trip to the stars would be an impossible mass hit. Magnetic shielding is a mass hit plus a power hit. So the bottom line is either create *Homo galacticus* or stay home."

"How long do you figure that will take?"

She shrugged. "Fifty... hundred years, maybe. That would be for a population to colonize the asteroids."

"So you'll probably never meet a real walking, talking *Homo galacticus*."

"Oh, I'll meet them, the first batch anyway. But they'll be children, not fully engineered for space. There's more to engineering a galactican than radiation resistance."

"Like what?"

"Like we don't need a population of football linebackers. Robots do the heavy lifting on a space station, so something the size and build of the Pygmy I mentioned would be more suitable—about 30 cm shorter than your linebacker. And we'd like them to be naturally sterile so they don't overpopulate their space stations—if reproduction becomes necessary, we'll make them temporarily fertile with hormone injections."

I had a thought. "How many people know about what you're doing?"

"I don't know. Management is informed. I'd say most of the crew and staff on *Einstein* are aware of it. We don't make a big secret of it. Why do you ask?"

"I'm just thinking out loud here, but what if the killer is some religious type who thinks what you're doing is immoral? Say he's deranged like religious types can be sometimes."

"Why kill a flight surgeon?"

"Terrorism? The victim was popular, pretty. Her death would get a lot of attention. Eventually *Einstein* would be facing a recruiting problem."

"Eventually? You think this won't be the last murder?"

"That's possible," I said.

Awkward silence while I looked at her and she looked at her drink, swirling the liquid around with her finger. Finally, she licked her finger, looked up, and said, "Well, the killer's given one part of the research a higher priority."

"What's that?"

"Imagine you're on a starship five years from home and five years from your destination. Population somewhere between 500 and a 1000. Violent behavior crops up in response to... to... whatever. Anyway, if the males start squaring off into rival gangs, the chaos could compromise the entire mission."

"Yeah, I can see that. You're gonna need cops. Like Masters at Arms in the old navies."

"Probably. Or we could genetically engineer a galactican population that does not resort to violence the way humans and chimps do."

"Violence is a gene?"

"Partly. There are a number of genes—MAO-A, CDH13, and some others—that set up a predisposition for violent behavior. If the subject also had a stressful childhood, say they were abused, they often become criminally violent."

"Can't you screen for that during recruiting?"

"Yes, but there are a lot of contributing factors. For instance bonobos, *Pan paniscus*, aka pygmy chimps, are non-violent compared to chimps and humans. They settle their differences with sex. They are also female dominant—opposite of chimps. And they do not exhibit sexual dimorphism—where males are larger and stronger than females. These could be good features for a crew stuffed into the cramped confines of a star ship for ten years."

"A matriarchy."

"Yes, but not an extreme one like, say, hyenas. I don't want one gender lording it over the other. I'd like a society genetically engineered for equality."

I snickered. "Sorry. I keep picturing a crew of chimps running a starship."

"Galacticans are gonna be people. At least they will be

when I get done with them. Meanwhile, I'm going to order three pairs of bonobos for evaluation."

I was silent a moment as I cradled my jaw in my palm.

"What are you thinking?" she asked.

"I'm thinking you've given me two motivational leads for our killer. First, we could have some loony up here who's trying to torpedo your research for the sake of fundamentalist religious or anti-eugenics views. That one's probably a long shot given how many loose screws this killer has, But I'll check it out. Second, in any small society with free love, like you appear to have on *Einstein*, somebody is bound to feel marginalized. That's a much likelier motivation. Except for the blood thing—that's just strange."

She downed her drink and I thought she was getting ready to leave so I changed the subject to stall her.

"You seem pretty fit."

"Mui Thai," she said with a shrug.

"You any good?"

"I don't compete any more. Just enough to take the edge off. You?"

"What?"

"You seem pretty fit yourself."

"Weights and treadmills. Pretty boring."

"No martial arts?"

"Used to box in the Army. Wasn't very good." I bent my nose over to show how it had been broken. She bent her broken nose back at me. We both laughed. Then there was that awkward silence again.

"Why don't you ask me what you really want to ask me?" she asked.

"Okay." I took a drink of Scotch, then leaned toward her. "You don't think this killer is a—"

She tilted her head toward me, eyebrows raised. "Seriously? That's what you *really* wanted to ask me?"

"Well, yeah. I mean I did a lot of homicide in the Army. Saw a lot of creepy shit. But this is straight outa some B-grade horror movie, especially being on a space station. Anyway, it would help my mental stability if I knew my partner didn't believe in space vampires."

She laughed. "Oh, I'm your partner now?"

"Why not? I could deputize you, if you want. Find you a little badge maybe."

"Do I get a gun?"

"A gun? Sure, same as me. You point your finger at the bad guy and say 'bang.'"

"What about the rest of the security force? Wouldn't they make better partners than me?"

"Not really. They're security types, not even an ex beat cop in the whole bunch, much less a gumshoe. Meanwhile, you got two things I'm gonna need to crack this: brains and a lab."

I downed my Scotch and stood up smiling at her.

"That mean you're spun down enough?" she asked.

"I got what I came for!"

"Whoa, there, Trigger! I didn't say I'd do it."

I sat back down. "Let me tell you how this is going down. First, this isn't a one-off. Creepy shit like this almost always means a serial killer. That means we're in a race—we gotta catch him before he drains his next victim."

"*Him*? You think it's a man?"

"Serial killers are usually men. But you're right, there's an outside chance it's a woman. Second, before I turn in tonight, I'm gonna file a report. At the end of the report, I'm gonna say I think it's a serial killer and that we need more security—with fire arms—and a full ten-person investigative team up here."

"Great, problem's gonna solve itself, right?"

"Not great. Even though I'm gonna milk the first-murder-in-space angle for all it's worth, they're gonna say 'no.'"

"No? How come?"

I let myself vent a little, "Cause they never give me anything I ask for. Cause they're way down there. Cause we're way up here. Hell, I don't know. They're bureaucrats! But trust me. Nothing is going to happen from their end until we have another murder, maybe two. So, we're probably going to lose the race. Did I mention serial killers leave very few clues? I can promise you this guy left some, but we weren't smart enough or equipped enough to pick 'em up. So, we have to spend our time between now and the next victim getting smarter and arranging to pick up on clues he figures we won't think of. Now," I leaned across the table toward her. "Will... you... help... me?"

She paused briefly. "Yes."

Captain's Office
Next Morning

"Did you know Jessica Maloney?" I asked.

"Not really. She was my flight surgeon," the captain said. "I'm flight crew. We try to avoid flight surgeons. Hadn't seen her in almost a year."

The captain's office was three meters' square, pretty large as rooms go on a space station. The desk—did I mention it was faux-wood? The desk faced people entering the room. Behind it was a panel of monitors showing various parts of the station plus a bunch of arcane digital readouts.

Captain Samantha 'Sam' King was a former pilot on the Space Only Shuttle *SOS Grouper* back in 2070. She was a compact, muscular, honey-colored brown woman who shaved her head to a no-nonsense sheen leaving a faint salt and pepper hue at the temples. Monica and Dr. Martin had managed to squeeze in with me as I briefed the captain.

She sat at her desk head tilted away from us, as she reviewed the report on her screen. She was trying to be stoic, but every now and then I could detect a faint wince as she got to a gory part. "You think the killer is a vampire?" she asked when she was done.

"Renfield's Syndrome," I said. "Vampire emulator."

"You've seen them before?"

"Not first hand. Just searching the criminal databases. Emulators like this one are rare, and they're almost always serial killers."

"Why almost?"

"Sometimes the perpetrators are captured after their first kill. So, nobody really knows what their intentions might have been after that."

"Okay, let's assume you're right—a serial killing vampire emulator. What do you need me to do? Bear in mind, this station is not just up here for good looks—we still have a mission to perform."

"I've requested a full ten-person investigative team from Earth. I expect to be told no. When that happens, I'd like it if you'd do a little ranting and raving."

"Okay, so let's say you get turned down and my ranting and raving are not as effective as you'd like. What then?"

"Then I'll need to draft maybe ten or fifteen of your people—full time—to help with data analysis. For example, there's hours of video data that can best be evaluated with the human brain."

"Okay, what else?"

"Dr. Carvalho and her lab—full time."

"Hey, wait a minute—you never said anything about full time! We've got experiments underway that need regular attention!"

"Find a way to do them in your spare time, Monica," the captain said. "This takes priority."

Monica nodded. "Ohhh-kay."

The way Monica dragged out the pronunciation of 'okay,' I worried I might have lost an ally.

"What else?" the captain asked, turning back to me.

"A war room? Some place we can lock up. Big enough to house about ten people and their work stations. Maybe a mini-war room attached where we can do interviews?"

"Got it. Next?"

"We need super tight control on who exits and boards the station—we need to quarantine ourselves, so to speak. And we need to keep everything we know and are doing under close hold, need-to-know only. We can't have the press tipping our hand to the killer, nor do we need the press spreading panic among the rest of the crew."

"Speaking of the crew, what should I tell them?"

"Tell them there's been a murder. Tell them we request everyone's full cooperation while the investigation is under way."

"Are we vulnerable, Mr. Stone?"

I hesitated. "Yes." I let the word hang there. Everyone just sort of stared at everyone else.

"Is there any way we can mitigate that vulnerability, Mr. Stone?"

"Yeah, now that you mention it. Put the whole station on a 7x24 buddy system. Nobody goes anywhere without his buddy—not even to the bathroom."

"That's not going to be easy," the captain said.

"What's easier? Suffering the inconvenience of a buddy system, or writing another letter home to somebody's next of kin?"

"What I meant was now I'll have to break it to the whole crew that we have a serial killer on the loose."

"I take your point. Maybe hold off on having everybody buddy-up in their rooms."

CHAPTER FIVE

After visiting the captain, I went back to my quarters to think and chill. The first thing that occurred to me was that doubling up in these tiny rooms would not be possible. Maybe if you did hot-sheeting like in the Navy on a watch-by-watch basis. I decided against it. Not only would it amount to a major inconvenience to everyone, there was little to be gained in security.

The crew up here was not military. SpaceCorp flight people were something in between military and civilian. Funny lot. They had rank, mostly among the astronauts, but referred to each other by their first names. Except the captain. Everybody called her Captain and she called everyone by their rank or title. Unless it was somebody like Monica—then it was first names both ways. Also funny, even among those who went by first names only, there was never any confusion about who was in charge, a kind of personality-meritocracy thing.

I logged into my email and found only a single letter, a response to my investigative support request. Technically, a 'request taken under advisement' is not the same as a 'no.' So, it looks like I'm stuck doing my own forensics. Might as well try to find that war room the Captain said I could have.

The Captain was as good as her word. When I showed up at the war room there were six shining faces smiling at me, computers tucked under their arms.

The war room was bigger than I expected. It looked about 4x5 meters with eight cubicles around the perimeter and a long table down the center.

"This place looks like it was pretty busy. How'd you manage to evict everybody?"

The shining faces stopped smiling and looked at the floor.

"We're the evictees," an Indian chap said. He stepped forward offering his hand. "My name is Mak Subramanian. I'm the shift leader for the ones you see in this room."

Mak, hmm... Being a New Yorker, 'Mak' should be easy to remember even if he didn't look Irish.

"We've been 'repurposed' as Captain King told us."

"I count six of you," I said.

"There are three more, but they're between shifts right now."

I made an attempt at levity. "I trust you all have alibis?"

That got them looking at each other.

"Alibis for what, Inspector?"

"You don't know what you're supposed to be doing?"

"No, Inspector. Just that we are to do your bidding until further notice."

"And we are to keep absolutely silent about it," an Asian woman said.

"Can you tell us what has happened, Inspector?" Mak asked.

"Inspectors are British. I'm a detective but you can just call me Roy. As to your question, there's been a murder, and I need your help to investigate it. You'll be examining hours of security files, going over personnel records, coming up with witness lists, doing preliminary interviews with witnesses. I'm the only one here with forensics training, at least for now, so I'll be the one examining the victim's room for evidence. Dr. Carvalho and her lab will be sifting through that evidence to see if it means anything. Questions so far?"

"Who was murdered... uh, Roy?" Mak asked.

"Flight Surgeon Jessica Maloney."

I started with the victim's room, instead of interviewing the dozens of crew she knew or associated with. Room evidence might go stale on me. On the other hand, witnesses might go stale too. Like so many things in life, it was a crap shoot.

I started with a small vacuum cleaner that I borrowed from housekeeping. I got a set of clean filter bags and labeled each one for where I would use it—bedding, sink counter, floor, etc. Hopefully, I might catch some clothing fibers or hairs that did not belong to the victim. Autopsy final report showed there had been no evidence of sexual entry either vaginal or anal. Hmm... Weren't Renfield perps sexually motivated? Have to research that. Maybe this goof was just in it for the blood.

Next step was to go over every surface that could hold a print with my print scanner. I already had the victim's prints in its memory, so if she had any visitors—welcome or otherwise—the scanner's comparator would surface them in a few seconds.

Bingo! Got a partial on a wine glass by the beverage cabinet. Odd, this goblet was the only stemware in the room. There were six regular tumblers in the dish rack by the sink. I taped a tag to the bottom of the glass and carefully dropped it in an evidence bag. Maybe Monica's lab could produce some foreign DNA from the partial. They'd only need a couple of skin or saliva cells, then Polymerase Chain Reaction or PCR could replicate the constituent DNA into a zillion copies of itself in a few hours.

That done, I went through the victim's personal effects. Her closet held the usual assortment of fitted coveralls in different colors. Everybody on the station wore them—I was the only oddball in jeans, track shoes, and a military style khaki shirt under a leather flight jacket. On Earth I used the flight jacket to cover my shoulder holster where I parked the snub-nosed .357 magnum that I liberated from the Army after The Dissolution. Up here there were no firearms of any kind allowed, but the jacket was still a comfort in the cool air of the station. I did manage to sneak my 23-cm Latama stiletto and my leather thumb sap through security. The Latama was a beauty that I'd won in a crap game in the Bowery when I was in high school. The blade tip was broken off but I managed to machine a new blade in metal shop along with some other wear-prone parts while I was at it. But if I was going to be here for a while, I'd better get some coveralls of my own. What I was wearing was going to start getting ripe soon. I felt under my jacket where the shoulder holster would have been. I missed my .357.

Jessica's dresser drawers had the usual assortment of underthings plus a few sweaters and scoop-necked t-shirts with clever doctor jokes on them. Hmm... Drop dead gorgeous yet she still feels the need to draw attention to herself. Small box of jewelry in the top drawer containing mostly earrings and a couple of chain necklaces. One locket with nothing inside. No false bottom in the box. I put her computer and communicator in evidence bags after I scanned the keyboard and case for prints. I'd let my geek squad back at the war room sort through unlocking the memory banks and figuring out if there was anything useful in them—that kind of task can be a real energy vampire... god, did I say that?

Lastly, I did a structural check of the room—floor panels, air vents, behind mirrors, under the mattress, pulling out drawers, and checking door latches and behind electrical switches and sockets. Nothing under the floor panels. Air vent screws seemed in good repair, but I took them out anyway. I used the peek-a-boo attachment on my scanner to look down the vent shafts. Nothing, and that was wrong. Air vent shafts always have a layer of gummed up dust. This one was pretty bare for about a meter in either direction. Odd. Maybe air on the station was super filtered and didn't have any dust floating around in it. Monica might know about that, running her clean rooms and all.

No evidence of tampering on the door latch. The door was not very heavy duty, good for privacy and not much else. Just like an ordinary interior door down on Earth except it was made of nanocellulose and it was airtight when closed. Latch was electric with a four-button keypad. Not high security. But this one also had a wifi button antenna that allowed it to be opened without the code. Probably for maintenance. People set the code to whatever and then checked out of the room without resetting it to all zeroes. Who did the maintenance around here anyway? Electrical switch covers and outlet covers were free of prints and showed no tampering.

I gathered up my bag of goodies and headed off to find Monica's lab.

Chapter Six

I found Monica in her lab drooping over her afternoon coffee. Maybe it was morning for her. Hard to tell up here with no sunrise and everybody working oddball shifts.

"Got any more of that stuff?" I asked.

She pointed to the pot on the counter. There were cups in the glass-faced cupboard above the pot. The stuff wasn't half bad. I put the evidence bag with the glass in front of her.

"What am I supposed to do with this?" she asked.

"I already scanned it for prints—got a partial. I'm wondering if you can pull off any cells for DNA?"

She held the bag up and spun the glass around. "We can try. Anything else?"

I pulled the vacuum filter bags out of my pack. "These came from various places around the victim's room. Can you examine the contents for fibers, hairs, cells, or whatever? We'll need photos of anything you get with a light microscope. If anything turns up, we'll need to compare it with other samples we gather around the station."

"So you'll want us to rig up a comparator microscope?"

"Yeah."

"Okay, what else?"

"That's it for now. I'm off to the war room to school my amateur sleuths in the dark art of forensics."

There were only three of my nine people on duty in the war room when I walked in. "Where is everybody?" I asked.

A short heavyset Asian woman I hadn't met before came forward.

"I'm Lijuan. Three people are off shift. The other three are at breakfast."

Her voice was husky. She held her hand out for me to shake. I took it, warm and fleshy. "Lijuan... beauty and grace?"

"You know Chinese?"

"Grew up near Chinatown."

"Ah, you are from San Francisco?"

"Manhattan, across from Roosevelt Park. Used to stop in at a pretty good dim sum shop on the way home from school."

I put the evidence bags with the victim's computer and communicator on the table. "Anybody here knows how to get these open—see what's in memory? By the way, what exactly did you guys do for a living before I showed up?"

"This is a CAD facility. We were designing engine mount structures for the Mars ship."

"Mars ship?"

"Yes, *SIS Pascal Lee*. It is supposed to depart in 2100."

"Mars, huh? Well, we don't want to hold that up. Any other progress?" I asked.

"You mean with the video hallway scans and people the victim associated with?"

"Yeah. Start with the video."

"We have a two-hour gap in the coverage at the time of the murder. We are guessing that's too coincidental for a random malfunction, so we are checking to see if there is a virus in the system."

"What about coverage in the days leading up to the murder?"

"We've gone back two months. There are several two-hour gaps—always when the victim is off shift. Where we have complete footage, it's mostly people who live on this wing. They come and go at shift change. The victim had a number of visits from one male visitor over the last two months."

"Good work. Got an ID?"

Lijuan looked at her notepad computer. She used a stylus and wrote in cursive. Maybe the computer knew what she was saying but I didn't.

"We think it is probably Juan Rodriguez. Shuttle pilot."

"Okay, what about other known associates?"

"Here are her listed patients—there are 341 of them. And another list of her co-workers—14 of them."

"Rodriguez a patient?"

"Yes."

"Good. Get him in here. He'll be our first interrogation."

"He's flying the circuit right now. Won't be back for a month."

"The circuit?"

"The space stations here at EML1 orbit about the Lagrange Point in a Lissajous orbit. It's shaped like a big potato chip about 50 thousand km in diameter. Each station takes about two weeks to complete the orbit. Shuttles fly a one-month circuit visiting each station to drop off passengers and cargo."

"When did Rodriguez leave?" I asked.

"The day before you got here."

"So he would have been here the night of the murder?"

"It appears so."

"Is there any way to put him in her room the night of the murder?"

"Not without the missing video."

"Would he have been working a shift?"

"Shuttle pilots don't work shifts like the rest of us. They get flights, they fly. The rest of the time they're off duty and they do as they please."

"Try interviewing the other pilots. Maybe they knew where he was. Can you get me some names?"

"Sure."

I left to find the Captain. Step one, I needed a search warrant for Rodriguez' room. Step two, I needed to apprehend him for questioning. Step three... for some reason I never make it to three.

"We don't do search warrants up here, Detective."

"All due respect, Captain, but I really do need to get in there."

She smiled from behind her desk. "Detective, this is a space station and I am her captain. This ain't no democracy. You want to go into Rodriguez' room, then I am authorizing you to go ahead and go. Turn the place upside down and inside out. The wing super should be able to let you in. Anything else?"

"Yeah, now that you mention it. I was told Rodriguez is thousands of klicks away on a supply run of some kind. How do I apprehend him for questioning?"

"Depends. Do you want to go get him, or do you want him to come back here?"

"I guess that depends. Which way is quicker without him becoming a flight risk?"

"Is he a suspect?" she asked.

"Not exactly. More like the only person on my most-likely-to-become-a-suspect list."

"Do you think he's a flight risk?"

"Only if he did it."

"Well, I can call the station captain at his next stop and have him apprehended and sent back on a scooter."

"Is that like a shuttle?"

"Smaller, a lot faster. One pilot, no copilot. Holds six passengers and a like amount of cargo. Every station captain has a couple of them at their disposal. While he's on his way back, you can search his room and talk to his colleagues—see if he has an alibi."

"You don't think he'll try to cut and run?" I asked.

"Not with the shuttle he's currently driving. It's not capable of Earth return."

"Then let's scoot his fanny back here!"

I spent six hours in Rodriguez' room. He had a big monitor on his desk. No computer—probably had it with him. No communicator either, same reason. No personal clutter. More like a crash pad than a place where somebody lived. If he was out for a month at a time when he had missions, maybe he had other crash pads. I wondered if he had a home at all. Surely he had some place to keep his personals. Maybe he just lived out of his duffel bag, like Patty.

Interrogation Room

I had left instructions with Lijuan to get Rodriguez' colleagues rounded up while I scrubbed his room. When I walked into the war room, there they were—well, two of them anyway. CisLuna maintained a stable of thirty or so shuttle pilots. Each one was home-based on a station.

I asked Mak to sit in to record and act as a witness.

Colleague #1 was Roosevelt 'Rosie' Jones, a tall, medium-colored black guy. Handsome, broad nose, lantern jaw, thick neck, broad shoulders and really long arms. I put him at 2 meters and change and maybe a bit over 100 kg. He moved like a boxer. Yeah, definitely a boxer. Unmistakable the way he moved his head from side to side on top of his shoulders like he was dodging a punch.

"Thank you for coming, Mr. Jones." I extended my hand. His grip was warm, dry, and very firm. I bet he could have squeezed water out of a cue ball.

"What's this about?"

"I'm not at liberty to say, but your cooperation is extremely important. I can get Captain King to back me up if you like."

His eyes shifted back and forth to Mak and me. "We need that camera?"

"I'm afraid so."

More silence, then he finally sat down, leaning back in his chair with his fingers laced across his midsection.

"Where were you two nights ago?"

He looked at the ceiling a few seconds, "Let's see... that'd be the gym."

"Anybody with you?"

"Yeah."

"Names, please?"

"Juan Rodriguez and some white girl."

"She have a name?"

"Most folks do."

Okay, I deserved that. "She share it with you?"

"Nope."

"Can you describe her?"

"Fit, medium build, like she worked out a lot."

"Hair color?"

He looked at the ceiling again. "She was a redhead. Yeah, lotsa freckles too. Had 'em everywhere."

"And you didn't try to talk to her?"

"Nah, man. Rodriguez did. I think he was trying to score."

"How long did you all stay at the gym?"

"They left after a couple of hours. I spent another hour in the lap tank."

"Where did you go after that?"

"Albert's for one a them no-cal beers."

"Did you meet anybody there?"

"Yeah. Jessica Maloney. She was at the bar. Joe was trying to get her to taste some new wine he got in."

"Who's Joe?"

"The bartender."

"How well did you know Jessica?"

He hesitated, shifting his gaze toward Mak and his camera.

"We fucked."

"You were lovers?"

"No, we just fucked."

"Did you go to her room that night?"

"No, she came with me to mine, stayed about an hour, then left."

"Did she say where she was going?"

"Nope."

"That was it? Just got up and left?"

"She said, 'Thank you.'"

"Okay, Mr. Jones, I'm sorry to have to ask you something so personal, but can you describe the sex act?"

"I figure that's between me and Jessica."

"Jessica's not with us anymore."

That shook him. After he took a second to do the math, he said, "She the dead girl?"

"Yeah."

"You think *I* did it?"

"Right now I'm just trying to put two and two and two together. Can you help us out? Did you use a condom?"

"Yes."

"What kind of sex did you have?"

"What? The fuckin' kind! What do you mean?"

"Was it vaginal?"

"Oh. Yeah, it was vaginal. Then we did the other kind. She wanted it in her ass. Said I had to use a new condom."

"No embellishments of any kind? Like bondage, say?"

"You mean did I tie her up? No. We fucked twice, then she left."

"After saying 'thank you.'"

"Yeah, after saying 'thank you.' We finished? Can I go now?"

"One more question, Mr. Jones. The wine that Joe gave her... did she finish it at the bar?"

"Yeah."

"She didn't take a half full glass with her back to your room?"

"Nope, no glass. She put it on a table as we were walking out."

Colleague #2 was Patty Eisenhower – yes, the same Patty assigned to babysit me on my ride out to CisLuna. She was cute and friendly as ever, nonplussed by the fact that I had recently seen her wiping her ass the other day and that today a stranger was holding a camera on her. We made chit-chat for a bit, then I got down to business.

"I suppose by now you know about the murder... Jessica Maloney?"

"Who doesn't?"

"Fair enough. Did you also know we're looking for Juan Rodriguez?"

"What, John-boy? You think he killed her? No way!"

"How do you figure?"

"He was nuts about her."

"Was he aware that she was two-timing him?"

"Two-timing him? More like five or six-timing! But yeah, he was aware."

"How do you know?"

"That he was aware? He used to talk to me about it in bed."

Statements like that made me wish I'd spent more time in vice. It was slowly dawning on me that space people were different than Earth people. Patty read the surprise on my face.

"Don't look so shocked, Roy. There's not much to do up here apart from working and eating and sleeping. We have to seek our own entertainment, so to speak."

She punctuated that last statement with a shameless come-hither smile. By now I was sure I was blushing.

"Are you suggesting I should forget the jealousy motive?"

"Who would he have been jealous of?"

"Rosie?"

"Nah, they were best buds."

"Buds enough to share Jessica?"

"Oh yeah. Besides when Jessica was flying Bravo, there were plenty of backups."

"Flying Bravo?"

"Huh? Oh, pilot talk. Uh... dripping crimson?"

I raised my brows. "Menstruating."

She winked her eye and pointed her index finger at me. "Yeah!"

"Do you have any names for these 'backups?'"

"Well, me when I'm not flying a circuit. Thing is, it's unusual for the three of us to be on the same station at the same time. *Einstein* is home station for each of us. But we mostly just live out of our flight bags. It's pretty much the same with all the shuttle pilots.

"So what about you and Jessica, were you friends... enemies... didn't give a shit?"

"That's a good question. Frenemies? Is that a word?"

"Used to be, I think."

"Put me down for 'don't give a shit.' She could be a bit superior at times. You know, her being a flight doc and me being just a shuttle jockey."

"Was she your flight surgeon?"

"No! Thank god."

"So there was some animosity?"

"No."

"You sure? Maybe you didn't like being the backup?"

"Please! I get plenty of action."

"You didn't give Rodriguez the idea to off Jessica while you were on Earth?"

"Fuck off, Roy!"

She laughed when she said that, so I knew there was no way to rattle her. I'd heard that it was almost impossible to manually dock a shuttle with a station if the flight control computer was out. It had only been done once... and that was by Patty. She was a very ballsy little gal.

"Can I go now?" she asked, her eyebrows raised.

I hesitated a moment. "Yes, you can go. Just don't divulge any part of this conversation to anyone."

She rose from her chair abruptly and stomped toward the door saying, "Yeah, right."

"Oh, and Patty..."

She stopped, her hand on the doorknob looking back over her shoulder. I hesitated, wondering if she should dye her hair to something besides blond.

"C'mon, Roy. I got a date."

I shrugged. "Sorry, go ahead then."

She turned and left, shutting the door behind her.

The next day Rodriguez was in the interrogation room wearing plastic bracelets to secure his wrists to a D-ring newly added to the top of the table. He didn't look happy, and I can't say I blamed him. The plastic bracelets were a bit much given we only wanted him for questioning. Have to remember to counsel the amateur cops on the other stations.

Meanwhile, we'd added some chairs around the table, making sure the suspect had one side of the table to himself. Lijuan, Monica, and I were in the other three chairs on the opposite side of the table. Lijuan was there to witness and video-record Rodriguez' statement. Monica was there in an apprentice capacity. I might need her to do preliminary interrogations if we started getting gobs of witnesses, but I didn't tell her that for fear she'd bolt.

Rodriguez scowled at us from across the table. I think he might have been there over an hour waiting. Even so, the last thing I wanted was to let Rodriguez think I was afraid of him. On the other hand, if he was afraid of *me*, that was okay. I reached across and put my left hand on top of his hands, holding them to the table, then pulled out my stiletto and snapped the blade open. I hesitated a couple of seconds fixing him with my beadiest detective stare, then slipped the blade into the plastic cuff on his right hand and cut it, freeing both his hands from the D-ring.

He looked down at the other cuff and asked, "You're not going to cut this one off?"

"Thank you for coming, Mr. Rodriguez."

He leaned back in his chair, cocky little bastard.

"Yeah, like I had a choice."

I gave him a snarky half-smile. "Let's start with my all-time favorite. Where were you two nights ago, Mr. Rodriguez?"

He thought a second, "In my rack."

"Did you go anywhere before you turned in?"

"Yeah, Rosie and I went to the gym."

"How long were you there?"

"Couple hours."

"Then what?"

"I went to my room."

"Alone?"

"Yeah."

"You didn't meet anybody at the gym? A little redhead, maybe?"

"Penny?"

"Yeah, she have a last name?"

"Probably."

I glared at him, saying nothing.

"She just said her name was Penny."

"Did you and Penny leave together?"

"Yeah."

"Whose room did you go to?"

"She went to her room. I went to mine. I was starting a shuttle circuit the next day."

"Did anybody see you enter your room?"

"What, you mean like my mommy came up to read me a story and tuck me in?"

"Yeah, something like that."

"No."

"What kind of wine do you drink?"

"What the... You drag me off my shuttle run to see what kind of fucking wine I drink?"

"Humor me."

"Fuck you! What's this about anyway?"

"Do you know Jessica Maloney?"

"Yeah."

"How well do you know her?"

"Pretty well, I guess."

"You ever drink in her room?"

"Yeah, sometimes. Loosen things up a little."

"Drugs?"

"I'm a shuttle jock. I gotta pass my whiz quiz, man."

I sat there staring at him to see if he'd sweat out something interesting. He came through.

"We..." he looked at Lijuan and Monica, then back at me. "Sex. We have sex once in a while."

"Just sex?"

"Yeah, just sex. What's with Jessica? She turn me in for some kind of sexual harassment? Let me tell you, man, she's the one invites me into her room! I don't force myself on her."

"When was the last time you had sex with her?"

He squirmed. "I don't know. Maybe a day before my flight."

"How long has this been going on?"

"Six months. A year maybe. We usually hook up whenever I'm deadheading on *Einstein*."

Lijuan adjusted herself in her chair but kept her recorder going. Monica just stared, flat affect—she showed real potential.

"What kind of sex?"

"What?"

"What kind of sex?"

"What the fuck kind of question is that?"

I leaned forward, keeping my voice very even. "I've had a very long day, Mr. Rodriguez. Please don't make me ask you again. What... kind... of... sex?"

He was squirming a lot by now. Couldn't tell if it was because of the two women in the room, or the line of questioning, or both.

"I don't know. The fun kind. What do you mean?"

"Describe it."

"You mean like what position?"

"Did you use protection?"

"Yeah."

"Were the two of you alone? No third parties?"

"No, just us."

"You're sure."

"Hell yes, I'm sure! What kind of kinky fuck you think I am?"

"I'm trying to find out, Mr. Rodriguez."

"We talked about maybe doing a three-way. We never did it though."

"Why not?"

"She was afraid of her reputation. Being a flight surgeon and all."

"Whose idea was it? The three-way."

"I don't know. Hers, I guess. Maybe I brought it up the first time, but she wouldn't let it go. She wasn't ready to go through with it, but she wouldn't let it go. Know what I'm sayin'?"

"Did you ever tie her up?"

"Tie her... Look, I'm done playing games, Detective. I don't answer no more questions until you tell me what this is all about."

"Okay. Jessica Maloney has been murdered and we are trying to figure out if you did it."

That stopped him. Stopped him cold. His face turned white as a week-old stiff.

"Jessica... murdered? Who would do such a thing?"

"My money's on you, Mr. Rodriguez."

"Well, it wasn't me! I mean she was getting a little kinky I guess. But still nominal."

He bent his head down into his hands and wiped his eyes.

"She was a nice girl. I mean fuck... lotsa girls like to get tied up!"

"How did you tie her?"

"Her hands to the headboard. But I kept the knots real loose so she wouldn't bruise."

His eyes were soaked with tears. Not sure if it was more from stress or remorse.

"You maybe try to suspend her from the ceiling, say?"

"I didn't kill her, man!"

About then, Monica passed me her communicator with a text message on it:

> Partial print and DNA results in from wine glass. Neither are from Rodriguez.

"Mr. Rodriguez, you are free to go, but please keep your whereabouts known to us at all times. Do not leave the station, and above all, do *not* divulge any part of this interrogation to anyone."

He got up and stalked toward the door, then came back.

"Can I get this fucking strap off my wrist?"

I opened my blade again and cut the strap. He glared at me one last time, then left and slammed the door.

I gave my partners a cool-down moment, then turned the conversation toward Lijuan and Monica. "Thoughts?"

Both women were silent.

"Is he really a suspect?" Monica asked.

"No. He's more like what we call a 'person of interest.'"

"Explain?"

"Well, we can place him with the victim the night she was killed. We can also postulate a motive—jealousy that she was sleeping with Rosie. Patty's statement doesn't back that one up though. But the biggest reason to eliminate him from the suspect list is that he and the victim appear to have had regular and vigorous sex."

"How does that eliminate him?" Monica asked.

"I do not believe our killer—if he's a serial killer—is capable of regular sex. Many serial killers are impotent. They ejaculate by stabbing the victim numerous times, the knife blade acting as a surrogate for an erect penis. I have an alternate theory that this killer may be so consumed by his Renfield's Syndrome that he is simply not interested in sex—all he wants is the victim's blood. He may think he requires it the way a vampire would, or he believes that if he consumes enough of it he will turn into a true vampire."

Lijuan mumbled, "That's sick."

I nodded, "Um-hmm."

"How sure are you of your Renfield theory?" Monica asked.

"I'm trying not to pick favorites right now. It's just a theory. I would have liked to have gotten to Rodriguez a lot sooner. If he was the murderer, he would have had a long ride back in that scooter to come up with a story. A lot of serial killers are wicked-fine actors. But for now, I think it's somebody else."

I looked at Monica.

"So if the partial and DNA are not from Rodriguez, who are they from?"

"The print is from Jessica. The DNA samples are from Jessica and the bartender at Albert's."

"Bartender would be Joe?"

"Joseph Ralston. Everybody calls him Joe. Maybe she was enjoying a drink there when the place closed, so she took it back to her room."

I cut her off, saying, "Actually, Rosie said she finished the wine and put the glass on the table as she walked out with him."

"So could we have a different glass? She stopped off somewhere and got another glass?"

"Maybe. By the way, did you know that Jessica was promiscuous?"

"Yeah, just about everybody up here is. Apart from work, there's not that much else to do."

"Okay, but was she promiscuous enough to finish with the guy she left the bar with, then go to somebody else's room, start a new glass there, and them take it with her?"

"I don't keep statistics, but yeah, she slept around. A lot. Who's pointing fingers?"

"Patty Eisenhower."

Monica laughed, putting her hand over her mouth. "Why, that little hypocrite!"

"Was there animosity between them?"

"Too strong a word. More like competition. They both used to steal each other's dates. Got to be a running joke at Albert's. We'd have little side bets on who was going home with whom."

I tilted my forehead toward her and raised my eyebrows.

"Don't go all Sunday school on me, Detective! This place isn't Disneyland. We have to make our own entertainment."

"So I keep hearing."

She harrumphed, looking pissed.

I broke the tension asking, "Could the simpler solution be that the glass we have in evidence is from a different day?"

Monica sat up, raising her finger, "Or the murderer picked it up at the bar and planted it at her room later that night when he killed her."

"I'm gonna need to talk to Joe." I looked over at Lijuan.

"On it," she said.

"Okay, what about trace residue in the glass? If she only rinsed it, maybe we can find molecules from something besides wine, like a slow acting roofy?"

"What's a roofy?" Lijuan asked.

"It's a date-rape drug." Monica said. "Somebody slips it in your drink to make you pass out. Then they have sex with you. When you wake up, you can't remember anything. Mostly."

"Ew!"

Monica looked back at me, "You're thinking that might be how the murderer got her unconscious so he could drain her?"

"Yeah, possibly. Cause of death is the biggest unresolved issue in this case so far."

"So what am I looking for?" Monica asked.

"Most date-rape drugs are derivatives of benzodiazepine. Flunitrazepam, aka Rohypnol or Hypnodorm. Both drugs have been around for decades. They used to be popular with the more predatory bar-flies and frat-boys. I'm not much of a chemist but I recall reading somewhere that it degrades in postmortem specimens to... I forget what. Anyway, maybe there are trace samples of blood from the victim's brain that didn't drain out? Also check her urine. You're looking for a pretty high concentration in order to establish cause of death. Something on the order of hundreds of micrograms per liter."

Monica was scribbling all this into her pad with a stylus as I recited what little I remembered about date-rape drugs.

When she finished, she looked up, "Looks like the old spectrometer is going to get a workout tonight!"

I was at the desk in my room ruminating over a long day of little progress. Early stage investigations almost always waste a lot of time ruling things out. Then I saw Ciccolella's text pop-up. "Roy Stone: EYES ONLY" I typed my password to open it.

> Roy—we had a similar serial killer down here before you arrived. Three primary victims over the span of a year and a half ending in July of 2072. Each one blond, attractive, ages from 28 to 31. First two lived alone. Found dead in their apartments, suspended by their feet, and drained of blood in a similar manner to the way you described with your victim. The third primary victim included a collateral death—her husband found dead in his bed. He still had all his blood—no puncture wounds. Bodies discovered by their two kids who were sleeping in the next room. Now sit down for the scary part. The husband was Bob Forsythe and he was the principal investigating officer on the case. None of the victims showed signs of a struggle or forced entry. We never determined primary cause of death. We never identified any suspects. Case moved to inactive status July of 2074. Investigation files attached. Good luck.
> —Chick

So our boy is not a rookie. I keyed in my response:

> Thanks, Chief. So far we've still working on cause of death. Currently checking out benzodiazepine family of date rape drugs. Will let you know what we find out.
> —Stone

Before I shut down, I sent out one more message.

Emily—I need you to dye your hair. I don't care what color you pick, just so you're not a blond any more. xoxo, Roy

Blond, attractive, 28 to 31. I should have told Patty to dye her hair. Am I just being paranoid? I started to key in her name on a message. Fuck it. She'd probably tell me to piss off.

CHAPTER SEVEN

I found Monica sitting in her lab nursing a steaming cup of black coffee. Beside her was a complicated looking contraption she called a GCMS, a gas chromatograph mass spectrometer. Behind her was a large 1x1.5-meter monitor with a bunch of sample results. Her eyes were bloodshot from having pulled an all-nighter.

"Whatcha got here, partner?" I said as I drained the rest of the pot into a cup and turned to walk over to her table.

She glared daggers at me. I turned back to the counter and began making a fresh pot. Her glare softened.

She heaved a sigh and said, "Well, for starters, we were in luck in that we kept the unused solution we used to pick up stray cells off the glass. And we also used distilled water to dissolve the residue in the bottom of the glass—sometimes minute amounts of saliva will collect down there. Got Joe's DNA on the outside of the glass and Jessica's on the outside and inside. So the next step was to put part of our water solution in the gas chromatograph oven and start heating it up. Constituent chemicals from the solution will evaporate off and then we can shoot them into the mass spectrometer to identify them from their masses."

"Okay, so what did you find?"

"Water, alcohol, saliva components, and grape components. No benzodiazepine derivatives of any kind."

"What about blood from the brain and residual urine from her bladder?"

"You wanted me to look in her bladder for urine? How novel!"

"C'mon!"

"'Sorry, it's been a long night—I'm a little punchy. Anyway, same story. We found blood components in the blood, piss in her urine, but no benzodiazepine derivatives."

"So she wasn't drugged?"

"Doesn't look like it. At least not with benzodiazepine."

I banged the side of my fist down on the lab table. "Shit! Then what the fuck killed her?"

"I don't know, but could I sell you a theory?"

"Hell, yeah, woman! Spill!"

"Okay, we have a dead body but no obvious cause of death apart from it having no blood. We rule that out as a primary cause of death because there was no sign of struggle and most folks would not calmly hang there and allow themselves to be drained of their blood. Hypnosis maybe? Bit of a stretch. So, what would kill her and leave no trace? Answer: gas asphyxiation. Methane and CO_2 would be the usual suspects.

Both gases are odorless and colorless. We would have found methane in her blood if she had any blood left. But with CO_2, even if she still had blood, there would have been little evidence of elevated CO_2. My money is on CO_2."

"Don't you have atmospheric monitors in the rooms?"

"Smoke alarms and carbon monoxide. CO_2 is monitored at central air vents as a check on the CO_2 scrubbers—they're set to hold CO_2 to 250 ppm."

"So there could be a buildup in an individual room and environmental systems wouldn't pick up on it."

"Right."

"Okay, we need a team: a physiologist to figure out how much concentration of CO_2 would need to be introduced into the room to cause unconsciousness and then death; an environmental engineer to figure out how to get that much CO_2 into the room and also how to purge it after the fact."

I started to leave, then turned back. "Good job, Monica."

She smiled and squinted one eye as she flipped me off.

When I arrived at the interrogation room, Joe Ralston was already there. He'd brought a thermos and a cup. When he saw me looking at it he held up the thermos.

"Coffee?"

"No thanks, I'm about coffee'd out."

He nodded back at me, eyes wary. "This about Jessica?"

By now, Jessica's death was all over the station, so I figured I'd just be square with him.

"Yes."

"You don't think I had anything to do with it, do you?"

"Not at this time. We just want to get the facts straight about Jessica's last night in your bar. Can you tell us about that?"

He raised his brows and stared down at the table before answering. Funny how some people look up and others down when searching for inspiration.

"She came in about an hour before closing."

"Was she alone?"

"Yeah, but that didn't last long. Never did with her."

"Okay, then what?"

"We chatted for a bit while she knocked back a couple of glasses of wine. She likes... liked wine."

"Did you suggest any particular wine for her to try?"

"Yeah, we got some new stuff in, a case of Burgundy from Earthside. She was eager to try it, but I only gave her a taste—stuff's hard to ship up here. Mostly we make our own wine. Anyway, she downs that and keeps licking the inside of the glass with her tongue—broad knew how to turn a guy on! I gave her a little more."

"You indicated someone joined her. Was that about then?"

"Yeah, Rosie walked in right about the time I gave her the new wine."

"Did he try any wine?"

"No, all the pilots ever drink is beer. Cheap and cold, that's all they want."

"Anybody else in the bar?"

"Um... no. Wait, there was one guy came in shortly after Jessica. Took a seat at a table."

"Did you recognize him?"

"Yeah, Simon. Don't know his last name. Quiet guy, a little creepy. He's one of the wing supers."

"How long did he stay?"

"He musta left after Jessica and Rosie. I didn't see exactly—I was busy washing my dishes so I could close."

"Did you see Jessica carry her wine glass out with her?"

"No, I was busy closing up."

"Do you recall getting your wine glass back?"

"Uh... no, now that you mention it."

"Could she have put it down on a table as she walked out?"

"Can't say. I didn't see any glasses sitting around—that's something I always check before I lock up."

"Could Simon have picked it up when he walked out?"

"Maybe. Don't know why he would have picked up an empty glass though. Souvenir, maybe? Maybe it had her lipstick on it or something? Like I said, the guy was a little... you know... creepy."

"Thank you, Mr. Ralston. That will be all. Please don't divulge any of this conversation to anyone."

"Yeah, sure." He stood up, then paused.

"Something else?"

"Nah. I just hope you catch the bastard what did this. Jessica was a lot of fun." He turned to go.

"Oh, one more thing, Joe. Were you and Jessica—"

"—Yeah, I wish. She went for the younger guys."

After Ralston left, I looked over at Monica and Lijuan. Lijuan passed me her tablet. Simon Crowne, Wing Superintendent, Deck 3, B Wing.

"HR shows he's been here for three years, but there's no record of him arriving."

"What do you mean?"

"There's no flight manifest with his name on it."

"Is that unusual?"

"I can check with HR, but yeah, I think they track that kind of thing."

I thought a minute.

"You want to get Simon in here next?" Lijuan asked.

"Check with HR first. Get me his whole history. I have something else in mind for Mr. Crowne."

CHAPTER EIGHT

I called a meeting in Monica's lab. The usual crew plus Captain King and the doc were there.

"I want to search Mr. Crowne's room when he's not in it."

"I told you before, you can search anybody's room you want, Detective. I want this asshole found yesterday! Copy?"

"Uh, yes, sir. But what I have in mind is a bit off the grid."

"How off the grid?"

"I also want to search the contents of his GI tract. It's a long shot, but if he's drinking Jessica's blood there might be leftover DNA from her blood cells hiding in his stomach or intestines."

"How you gonna pull that off?" the captain asked.

"I was thinking if we induced some kind of disease symptoms that would justify the flight surgeon pumping his stomach and flushing his lower GI tract?"

Dr. Martin said, "That's do-able, but is that who we are? I mean, I realize this is not a democracy up here, but how sure are you this man is the murderer?"

I motioned to Lijuan and Mak to present their evidence.

Lijuan spoke first. "Simon Crowne, age 40, arrived on *Einstein* June 2083, no listing on any shuttle manifest."

The captain interrupted. "What? Then how'd he get here?"

"Could he have been a transfer, say, from another station, then rode over here on a scooter or something?" I asked.

"Nope. Nobody gets on my station without me knowing how they got here."

I looked at Mak who referred to his pad. "I've checked personnel records at Vandenberg. There are no records of anyone named Simon Crowne in their files. We also attempted a photo match using Mr. Crowne's ID photo. We found a possible match between him and a Mr. Austen Miller who transferred to *Einstein* in June of 2083."

He projected two images side by side onto the wall. They were vaguely similar, Miller's face obscured by a heavy beard and mustache.

Mak continued, "But according to our records, Mr. Miller never got here. His last known whereabouts were on the LEO space station *SSS Nathalie Cabrol*. Apparently, he debarked from his shuttle onto *Cabrol* and was never seen again. On the other hand, Mr. Crowne did arrive here about that time. We just don't know how."

I said, "To your point, Dr. Martin, I'm *not* sure if Simon Crowne is our man. But as I said before, we're in a race. Whoever the murderer is, he will kill again. And we have to stop him before that happens."

The captain said, "Dr. Martin, I'm not saying I'm going to approve this procedure, but how would you go about it?"

Dr. Martin thought a moment, then said, "We could introduce a concoction of ipecac for nausea, plus some kind of fever-inducing agent—I'd want to research that, maybe throw in some kind of antihypertensive—drop his blood pressure, make him woozy. Then we tell him there's a suspected outbreak of botulin poisoning, make up some story about how a dozen people have come down with it and one of them identified him as standing next to them in the cafeteria serving line. Then we haul him into sick bay, stick an IV in his arm and knock him out the rest of the way. While he's out, we run a tube down his throat and another one up his rectum and vacuum out everything in between. When he wakes up we fuss over him for barely surviving his 'close call' and compliment ourselves for catching it just in the nick of time."

The captain asked, "Would there be any lasting effects?"

"None."

"Monica, can you separate out any of Jessica's DNA from that mess?"

"Yes, sandwich immunoassay techniques can be set up to latch onto Jessica's DNA only. We have plenty of her DNA samples to formulate an epitope that will glom onto one of Jessica's unique genes. The trick is to pick out genes that are unique to Jessica and not Mr. Crowne. We'd need to sequence his DNA as a control—make sure Jessica's unique genes really are unique."

The captain asked, "How long would you need to keep him down for all that?"

Dr. Martin said, "We could drain his GI tract in an hour and put him back in general circulation a few hours after that—once we get his fluid levels and vitals back to nominal. Monica could take her time after that."

Monica said, "That's good. I'd want my lab crew to have a couple of days to be sure of our results."

The captain asked, "What are the odds you'll find viable DNA in his GI tract?"

Dr. Martin said, "Depends on how long it's been there. A day, maybe two. That's about how long DNA should last in the bowel after passing through the stomach enzymes."

I shrugged, "Like I said, it's a long shot."

The captain thought a moment, pursing her lips and shifting her gaze between Monica and Dr. Jones.

"Monica, you lost me at sandwiches, but I think you two know enough about what you're talking about to pull this off."

"All due respect, Captain, but am I the only one here who's read the Bill of Rights?" Dr. Martin asked. "We're not even sure this guy's a serial killer. I mean, the victim was, you know, pretty fast and loose with the guys. Couldn't this just be one of her lovers got jealous?"

I decided it was time to play my trump card. "Yes, it could be a case of jealous rage—I put that at under five percent probability. But that's not all. Jessica was not his first victim."

I projected the email I'd gotten from him the other night onto the wall.

"This is from my boss, Carmine Ciccolella. He's Chief of Police at Vandenberg."

Roy—we had a similar serial killer down here before you arrived. Three primary victims over the span of a year and a half ending in July of 2072. Each one blond, attractive, ages from 28 to 31. First two lived alone. Found dead in their apartments, suspended by their feet, and drained of blood in a similar manner to the way you described with your victim. The third primary victim included a collateral death—her husband found dead in his bed. He still had all his blood—no puncture wounds. Bodies discovered by their two kids who were sleeping in the next room. Now sit down for the scary part. The husband was Bob Forsythe and he was the principal investigating officer on the case. None of the victims showed signs of a struggle or forced entry. We never determined primary cause of death. We never identified any suspects. Case moved to inactive status July of 2074. Investigation files attached. Good luck.
—Chick

"Draining a guy's stomach under false pretenses may not be who we are, but it's who we need to be."

Monica and I were sitting at Albert's Bar when the captain walked in. She waved but took a table off to the side. Monica got up to see if she wanted company. The captain smiled and waved me over. I gathered up Monica's and my drinks and joined them.

"I've been communicating with Earthside for guidance about this case," the captain said. "I asked for a judge to try the case when we catch the guy—they said no, I'm the captain, I get to be the judge. Then I asked how I'm to deal with the felon—should we send him or her Earthside to stand trial? They said no, I'm the captain, I have to deal with him up here. I then asked if they had any guidance in that regard. They said only to ensure the felon can never commit any murders again. Oh, and they said one more thing, 'Do not add to the space debris problem.'"

"How do you feel about all that?" Monica asked.

The captain thought a moment. "I got a space station to run and they run better if there are no murderers on them. So I guess my biggest, hell, my *only* concern is that we get the right person. I don't want to execute an innocent man."

Monica and I looked at each other. "So you don't care how we get the evidence so long as it's irrefutable?" she asked.

"You planning to torture a confession out of him?" the captain asked.

"Tortured confessions are refutable," I said.

The captain drummed her fingers, then took a sip of whatever she was drinking. It was darker than Scotch, probably bourbon. "Tell me something, Stone."

"Okay."

"I know you're a cop, but why are you finding it so easy to abandon due process and all? I thought that was drilled into you."

"That's right."

"So what gives?"

"I guess I'm a special case."

If I'd hoped she'd leave it at that, I was wrong.

"C'mon, spill. What's your story?"

I sighed, then took a long sip from my Scotch. "Back when I was in the Army, I was part of their Criminal Investigation Division, CID. Homicide. Pretty good at it too. Most of the time it was just some goof killing somebody in a bar fight or while they were in the middle of a crime. One-offs. I only worked one serial killer—that'd be 2069. He liked to garrote his victims. Always left his apparatus around the victim's neck—his signature. Anyway, I guess you could say he made it personal for me."

"Go on."

I downed my Scotch and signaled Joe for another. "I started getting close to cracking the case when I got an anonymous letter saying to back off or there would be consequences. Well, that's the wrong thing to say to a homicide detective. To this day I wonder if he was counting on that when he sent that letter. Anyway, one day I came home and found my wife and child in the bedroom. My wife— her name was Hanna—was bound, gagged, and garroted.

Most of her hair had been cut off. My son—he was two. He was not bound or gagged. Presumably that was so my wife had to watch our baby being murdered in front of her eyes. The bastard left me a note. 'Told ya so, Stone!'"

Monica gasped and covered her mouth with her hand.

The captain looked embarrassed. She put her hand on my arm and shook her head like she wanted to say she was sorry but no words came out.

I shrugged, "Anyway, that's my story."

"Did you get him?" Monica asked.

"No. They pulled me off the case—admin leave. Couldn't say I blamed them. I was, uh, not entirely objective at that point. Had to watch from the sidelines—insult to injury. Eventually, they found the body of a guy they thought was the perpetrator. No positive ID on the body. No idea who that poor fool was. Meanwhile, the real murderer skipped town."

"You sound pretty sure about that," the captain said.

"For the rest of the time I was in the Army, up until 2072, I would get love notes from him. Always on the anniversary. 'How's the wife and kid?' He always stuck a lock of my wife's hair in the envelope. He liked blonds."

"Do you think this guy might be the same one who murdered your family?" Monica asked.

I looked down at the table and steepled my eyebrows, then looked up at Monica. "That thought has crossed my mind."

CHAPTER NINE

I was at Crowne's door but he wasn't answering.

I called Lijuan, "He's not here and I can't raise him on his communicator."

"Sometimes the supers work in some pretty remote places on the station, no coverage. You want to page him?"

"Nah, just get me his door code."

While she was running that down, I paced outside, wondering if there was going to be a surprise waiting for me when I got that door open. She called back, "6-34-5."

"Thanks, hang on while I try it and see if it works." I did and it didn't. I closed my eyes a few seconds and tried to count to ten. I only made it to two. That's as far as I ever get.

"Okay, get me an engineer. Tell him to bring something that can cut a hole in nanocellulose."

I was about to hang up when I had another thought, "Tell him to bring a drill and one of those fiber optic inspection rigs."

"Will do, boss." She had taken to imitating Mak calling me 'boss' all the time. Cute. I sat down on the floor and leaned against the wall, arms across my knees.

A couple of people passed by in the hour it took the engineer to get here. They both had the same question, "Locked out?"

"Yeah. Engineer's on his way."

Then they'd smile and move along.

The engineer was a middle-aged fellow named Dieter. Agreeable enough, but he looked like he could handle himself and had done so a time or two in his past.

I had Dieter poke a hole in the door with his drill. Then we inserted his fiber optic scope through the hole in case Crowne had rigged up any nasty surprises for trespassers. We spent twenty minutes checking out the room with his fiber optic gear. I was getting a bad feeling. Nobody keeps their room this neat, especially not a super. I figured we were blown and Crowne had skipped out for a new room somewhere. Maybe he left us some nice prints, perhaps something we could get a DNA sequence from.

"Okay," I said to Dieter, "let's crack this safe."

He grinned and had the door open in under a minute.

Inside, the room hadn't just been wiped. It had been scrubbed, scoured, and sterilized. I couldn't find so much as a pubic hair in the bed linen.

"Who the fuck lives in a room and doesn't leave any prints?"

Even the toothbrush was useless. The bastard had taken his old one and put a new one in its place, still in the plastic wrapper. The drawers were bare, not a stitch left behind. Laptop gone. Communicator gone. The guy had either moved out or never moved in, but where the devil was he?

A day later, I was back in the war room busying myself with pacing. I've never been good at waiting, especially when other people are doing the work.

We had put up APBs with Simon Crowne's picture posted on all the news channels on the station. We included a warning not to approach him if he is seen. We advised anyone who does see Crowne to contact me immediately. Then I kicked back in the war room and waited while everyone else was out rattling *Einstein's* rooms and corridors. Frustrating.

I paced around the war room some more. I did pushups. I practiced throwing my blade at a target I had rigged up on the wall away from the door. My basic drill was to detach my knife from the clip on my belt, flip it open, and throw it at the target letting the handle slip through my grip. The knife doesn't flip end-over-end that way. It's the fastest most accurate way to let the air out of a perp out to about five meters. Without my .357, throwing my knife was the only long range option I had. I had my thumb sap, but hey, nobody throws a sap. I wished I had two blades.

The target was a thick sheet of nanocellulose, the tough-as-nails shit they used to make everything on this station. The blade went in a good four centimeters pinning the plate to the wall. Try as I might, I couldn't get the damned thing out. It was in there good, plus it was up high and awkward to reach. I must have been more frustrated than I realized.

I tried doing some hand-stand pushups. I used to be pretty good at them when I was younger. After about five of them, I sat back down at the table and stared at my communicator, willing it to buzz, light up, anything. For something that was supposed to be so damn smart, it picked a fine time to dummy up on me.

I went back to trying to get my blade out of the target. I was standing on a chair and had just managed to get my fingers under the bottom edge of the nanocellulose target when Mak walked in and startled me. I jerked around as the target came loose and the chair toppled all at the same time. I was lucky I didn't skewer myself on the pointy end sticking out through the back of the target.

"We found a possible hideout, boss. You okay?"

"Yeah, I think so. Let's go."

"What about your knife?"

I looked down at the nano-target, but didn't say anything.

"The machine shop is on the way to the hideout. We can stop by there and they can pull your blade out without breaking it."

"Thanks."

CHAPTER TEN

It was a hideout all right. Obviously, it had been lived in, but by whom? I decided to start with the floor boards this time, hoping the change of procedure would change my luck. My head was down between the joists when I felt something pat me on the butt. I jerked my head out banging it on the floor board in the process.

It was Lijuan.

"What's up?" I asked, rubbing my head.

"There's been another murder, boss. You need to come."

"Who was it?"

"I don't know. They just said to get you."

"Okay, where is it?"

"Deck 2, B Wing."

"Those are crew rooms, right?"

"Yes."

"Anybody there?"

"Monica. She's got the whole wing locked down. Nobody gets in or out."

"Any security folks there?"

"Don't need 'em. Monica's tromping up and down the hall with her mad-bitch-from-hell face on. Everybody's too scared to even come out of their rooms to pee."

Monica was waiting by the victim's door when I got there. She already had on her bunny suit and slippers and offered me a set to follow suit. She did not look happy.

"Who is it this time?" I asked as I was getting into my suit and pulling on the slippers.

She didn't answer. She just opened the door and held it open for me. As I walked into the room, it was a familiar MO—blond, female, nude, suspended upside-down from the ceiling. Her back was toward me. I walked around to her front, taking care not to touch her body in the cramped confines of the room, hoping it would be someone I didn't know.

It was Patty.

CHAPTER ELEVEN

Autopsy Room

Dr. Martin was doing the autopsy again. I worried that working on people he knew from the station was taking a toll on him, but he soldiered on the way doctors have done for centuries.

He spoke into his microphone. "Victim's Name: Patricia Eisenhower. Caucasian female. Age 35. 158 cm. Weight 48 kg. Hmm... that's 4 kg less than her last recorded weight."

He mopped his brow with a towel and tossed it back onto the stainless-steel table by his side. "Again, that would be consistent with a complete loss of blood."

He walked around the corpse and spread the legs with Monica's assistance. "Victim's genital and anal regions are completely shaved. No evidence of foreign pubic hair."

Then he probed the vaginal and anal cavities with a long cotton swab. Each time they came out dripping with semen. He clipped off the ends of his swabs into separate test tubes and stoppered the ends, taking care to label each one with

Patty's name, the orifice he got them from, and the date and time of the sample extraction. He turned his head toward the microphone. "Victim has copious amounts of semen in the vaginal and anal cavities."

That's when I left. I knew the rest of the story and didn't need to hear it again.

Mak and Lijuan were alone in the war room, puzzling over their computers. I put my index finger over my lips to silence them and motioned them to come outside.

Out in the hall, I whispered, "I think this bastard may have bugged our war room. Mak, can you figure out how to sweep the room for bugs?"

He thought a moment, then said, "Sure, boss."

"Better sweep my room and Monica's lab as well."

I turned my attention to Lijuan, "I'm also worried that our text communications are being compromised. Can you determine if there are any eavesdropping viruses on the network?"

She smiled, relieved that I hadn't left her out. "Sure, boss!"

"Oh and Lijuan, you better find another way to snoop around the network besides your own computer—it's probably dirty."

*   *   *

I'll say one thing for Patricia Eisenhower, she was a popular girl. At least with one guy.

I found dark hairs on her pillow, dark pubic hairs lower down under the bed linen, prints all over the glasses, prints on the medicine cabinet mirror.

I looked at the dark hairs in the evidence bags. I knew whose they were without even testing them.

Juan entered the interrogation room flanked by two security men. His hands were cuffed with nano-ties. After they deposited him in his chair, they backed off to a discreet distance.

He did not wait for me to start the questioning. "Mr. Stone, I didn't do this!"

"Mr. Rodriguez, we have a lot of evidence to the contrary. We can place you in the victim's room the night she was killed. We have evidence to show you two were intimate." I showed him the evidence bags with the test tubes of semen on cotton swabs. "Very intimate."

"That don't mean I killed her! Why would I do such a thing?"

"A good Earthside prosecutor would have an easy time establishing a jealousy motive. *'Ms. Eisenhower was a regular sex partner with Mr. Jones.'* It wouldn't be hard to make that stick."

"Speakin' of prosecutors, don't I get a lawyer?"

"You would if we were Earthside, but as the captain has pointed out to me numerous times, *'We ain't Earthside and this ain't no democracy!'*"

"What's she gonna do to me?"

"If she becomes convinced you did it, I believe she will execute you."

"Execute me? How?"

"I don't know *how*, Mr. Rodriguez, but she is a very creative woman."

"Help me out, man. How close is she to thinking I did it?"

"We haven't presented her with the evidence in the Eisenhower death, but I would guess your intimate proximity to both victims is not going to play well with her."

"Ah shit, man. Look, I may have had sex with those women, but I didn't do it. I loved them. *Both* of them. I wanted to have *more* sex with them. I didn't mind sharing them with Rosie. Hell, there's plenty to go around for everybody!"

"That, my friend, along with the fact that we can't seem to find the other suspect, is probably the only thing keeping you alive right now."

We placed Juan in a makeshift brig, a 'luxury' cabin with a full bathroom and a kitchenette. I had the engineers attach two hasps on the door onto which we placed two high-security mechanical padlocks. I toyed with assigning a guard,

then decided there was a limit to the paranoia I would permit
myself on this case.

CHAPTER TWELVE

Captain's Office

"Captain, if Mr. Rodriguez is the killer, he can't hurt anybody while he is in custody."

She stared at me unblinking for about ten seconds. "Tell me again why you think he did it."

"I *don't* think he did it. But the evidence to indict includes putting him at the scene of the crime in close temporal proximity both times."

"English please."

"He was there at roughly the same time as the murder. That doesn't mean he was there at exactly the same time, but close."

"Okay, what else?"

"He has a history of intimacy with each victim, and in Patty's case it was the same night. So, if you couple that with a possible jealousy motive—Rosie Jones—you can make a case that he murdered them to get back at Rosie. A sexual turf war, so to speak."

Monica joined in saying, "But you have no evidence of jealousy. Juan and Rosie, at least in public, were always best buds."

"Besides," I added, "if he was jealous of Rosie, it stands to reason that he would take out Rosie, not the two women he was enamored of.

"But," I continued, "my biggest issue with Rodriguez is that he doesn't match the personality profile I have in my head for this particular serial killer."

"And what profile is that?"

"This guy is a loner, serious introvert, the type who held up the wall at the high school prom. Watched and coveted beautiful women. Always afraid to approach them. Maybe he did once back in his distant past but he botched it and was humiliated. Hence, he goes for the ultimate act of control. He steals that which made them passionate—their blood. The Renfield Syndrome looks like a close fit. If you recall from the vampire movies, when Dracula subdues his victim it's always a lustful act of ultimate control. He forces the act but the woman plays the willing victim. I'm not saying these gals were willing—he did kill them before draining them. But who knows what's going on in this perp's head when he's committing his crimes?"

"Speaking of Dracula, what about pumping Rodriguez' stomach for blood?" the captain asked.

"He's scheduled for that this afternoon. But I remind you, finding Patty's blood in his stomach or GI tract may prove his guilt, but *not* finding any blood does not prove his innocence."

"How's that?"

"He may have collected the blood but planned to consume it later. Or for all we know, this killer is not a Renfield type at all. He just drains the victim's blood and throws it away. Serials are always nutters in some way, shape, or form.

"And my last concern is that our best suspect, Simon Crowne, seems to have disappeared. We don't know why. We found what we think are a couple of his alternate hideouts, but we can't prove they were specifically *his* hideouts. It's entirely possible Mr. Crowne may have changed his identity."

"Changed it how?"

"Adopted a new name, a new disguise, a new role somewhere else on the station. Or he may have snuck onto an interstation shuttle and he's no longer on *Einstein* at all."

She fixed me with another one of her long unblinking stares. "Your reasoning, Mr. Stone, reminds me of a plate of spaghetti that stayed in the pot too long."

"Welcome to my world."

She rose, indicating the meeting was over.

"You have thirty days. If you don't find anything to either clear Rodriguez or convict someone else, I'm going to execute him."

Chapter Thirteen

War Room

"We have bugs, or had them anyway," Mak said.

"Where are they now?"

Mak held up a jar with nothing in it.

"You trying to be funny?"

"No, boss. This jar is RF-opaque. The bugs are down there in the bottom—microscale. You have to look real close."

I did and sure enough, in the bottom were maybe a dozen tiny little black beads.

"How'd you find them?"

He held up a gadget that looked like scanner of some sort. "I had Electrical build me one of these down in their shop. It's super sensitive, even picks up frequency-hopping, spread spectrum signals."

"Impressive."

"We scanned your room and Monica's lab and the interrogation room and the captain's office—they all came up nil."

"Great work, Mak." He beamed at my compliment.

"Lijuan, now that we can talk, what about viruses?"

"We have viruses all over the net, and while I was able to eliminate a bunch of them, there are about a dozen of them that auto-replicate every time I destroy them. Those are the ones I'm most suspicious of."

"What do they do?"

"Some of them intercept message traffic—I call those daemons. Each one seems to be designed to intercept just one target. It sends the message to a drop box that gets emptied now and again, but I can't actually look inside the drop box—it's behind some kind of firewall."

"Nasty. I can guess who the targets are."

She smiled. "You seem to be pretty popular, plus Monica, Rogers, me, and Mak. And get this, every time one of us sends a message to someone, it manufactures a new daemon to sit and watch for back-traffic from the new recipient."

I leaned back in my chair and ran my fingers through my hair giving my head a nice scratch in the process. "You said some of them. Are there more?"

"Yeah, there's standard viruses for turning on and off corridor security cameras and another neat one that jimmies with door codes. And last but not least, there's a neat one that grants the hacker access to personnel files on board the station."

"You think that's how he's changing his ID?"

"Yes, I do."

The captain's office

"How long you been up here, Stone?"

The captain looked like she could chew through steel bolts.

"I dunno, few weeks maybe. Time flies when you're having fun."

"Yeah, tell that to the two dead bodies!"

"Yeah, well I would, but they're not listening much these days."

"Don't get flippant with me, Stone!"

I leaned forward a bit. "And don't you play holier than thou with me, Captain."

"What do you mean?"

"I mean it's hard to catch a bad guy when he, she, or it can see your every move. Your fucking station is about as secure as... well, let's just say it's not secure. The guy scatters micro-bugs anywhere he pleases. And how does he get in? Easy, he has a virus on your net that lets him jimmy the door codes whenever and wherever he wants. He walks the halls with impunity because he has another virus that lets him turn off the security cameras whenever he feels like it. He changes his electronic identity at will with yet another virus that lets him into your personnel registry, not to mention eating in any cafeteria he wants under any identity he wants. Shall I go on?"

The captain was spared having to answer when Mak stuck his head in the door without knocking.

"There has been another murder."

"Oh, Christ!" I shook my head in dismay and got up to leave. "Take me to it."

"I can't. It's on *Borucki*."

PART II

Chapter Fourteen

Hangar Bay, *SSS William Borucki*

Once we were secure onboard *Borucki*, I sent Monica and the team on ahead to play meet-and-greet with the captain, James Nation. I'd heard he was big on protocol. I needed time to have a look around the hangar bay. Something told me I might find a clue as to how the bastard got here without *Einstein* knowing he left or *Borucki* knowing he arrived.

The little interstation shuttles don't use nuclear thermal rockets so it's safe to poke around their ass ends where the nasties come out. Instead they rely on plutonium heaters to superheat LH2 which then gets squirted in whatever direction you want to make thrust. There didn't seem to be anything unusual looking on the outer hull of the shuttle— not that I could tell the difference between usual and unusual anyway. So, I picked my way back into the shadows.

Stashed behind some large metal-looking boxes—I lacked the expertise to tell what they were—I found a large box that could only be described as a coffin. I tried to pick it up and found that it moved easily. I thumped the lid with my knuckles and it felt very solid, like heavy gauge sheet metal. I figured it must be made of carbon fiber. It was heavier than anything a woman could pick up—except for maybe Monica—but not so heavy that a strong man couldn't pick it up. The lid was secured with a pair of latches that could be opened from the inside or the outside. It had no locking mechanism and opened easily. The inside was padded and had LOX bottles secured in various places. And what looked like dirt, some kind of organic soil, lay in the bottom.

"The crazy bastard really *does* think he's a vampire."

Captain James Allen Nation's office

The sign on the door said, 'James Allen Nation, Captain, *SSS William Borucki.*' I could hear someone ranting inside. This must be the place. I didn't knock, just turned the handle and walked in.

"Are you Stone?" the captain asked.

"Yes."

"Well, if your tardiness is any indication of your inability to follow simple orders, I'm not surprised you've allowed this Crowne person to stow away on my station. And now see what's happened! A valuable crew member, part of the *Borucki* family, has been murdered in a most horrendous way! What have you to say for yourself, Mr. Stone?"

"The murderer's name isn't Crowne anymore."

"So what is his new name, Mr. Stone?"

"We don't know yet, but whatever it is, you won't find it on the manifest of any recent flights that arrived here."

"Mr. Stone, I already know I have an intruder on my station—I have a dead body to prove it. That you walk in here and tell me you don't know his name does me little good."

"I know how he got onto your station."

War Room on the *Borucki*

The new digs were the same form factor as our war room on *Einstein,* only this one hadn't been used as a design center. *Borucki*, as I'd learned, was where the Lunar surface crews deadheaded when they weren't working on the surface. Due to the low one-sixth gravity on the moon, crews could only take about a month at a time down there before their bones started to crap out. So, they hauled them back up for two month's recuperation in *Borucki's* full gee.

"So spill, Stone." Monica said. "What the fuck made you decide to look around the hangar bay?"

I shrugged. So, it's 'Stone' now.

"This sort of thing happens sometimes in homicide after you've been on a case for a while, especially if you've been coming up dry. After we got off the shuttle, I just got a hunch, like I could feel the bastard watching us right there in the hangar bay. Only a really dumb cop ignores his hunches in this business. Besides, if it was fruitless, I'd just get yelled at for being late to some captain's meeting." I flashed her my cavalier grin. "Hell, I've been yelled at before!"

Everybody seemed to think that was pretty funny.

"Okay, where's the coffin now?" Lijuan asked.

"Still there, but I emptied the LOX bottles that were full. If he tries to get away again, he won't survive the trip."

"What if he checks the bottles?" Lijuan asked.

"Yeah, don't they have gauges?" Mak asked.

"I scattered them around, so it should be pretty obvious somebody's been messing with his equipment. Besides, he's probably rigged some kind of telltale to warn him if somebody's been fooling with his ride. Anyway, I probably tripped it."

"So then what?" Monica asked.

"So then we complicated his departure a little—he'll have to make arrangements to get more LOX. Even so, I put an RFID under the padding—a little cheap insurance. If he goes back and moves the coffin, say, attaches it to another shuttle, we'll know about it."

"So you figure to recall the shuttle if it takes off with the coffin attached?" Mak asked.

Monica brightened, "Or maybe you could *not* recall the shuttle, just have a welcoming committee waiting for him at the other end. And if he failed to check his bottles, we'd be done with him."

I nodded, "We could do that. But what if it's not our boy? Say, he's somebody just decided to joyride between stations. I don't know... has a girlfriend or something. Listen, team. I want this guy as bad as you do. But I want the right guy."

Everyone looked glum after my morality lecture.

"Jessica and Patty were crew," Lijuan said. "Jessica was nice to me. She didn't have to be. I mean I'm not much to look at, but she was still nice to me." Her eyes got wet and she rubbed the tears away with one of those nanocellulose tissues she always carried in her sleeve. "I wouldn't mind if her killer suffocated between stations."

"I feel you, but I'm a cop, not an executioner."

I gave them a second to process that one, while I feigned setting up my computer.

"Okay, team, let's get down to business. Marty, Monica— I need autopsy results as soon as you can. I'm heading off to search the victim's room. By the way, do we have a name for the victim?"

Martin looked at his screen, "Melody Marks, age 29. She was a flight nurse."

I shook my head, "No wonder the local medics didn't want to raise their hand for this one. Okay, Lijuan, I need you to get busy filtering the personnel files to determine if there is anyone on the station who shouldn't be here—extant crewmembers with no valid arrival record, that sort of thing. What's the one thing that you absolutely have to have an ID for to function on a space station?"

Lijuan shrugged, "I can think of two things."

"Okay, shoot."

"Eating in the cafeteria and occupying a room."

"What if he's not using a room? Just found himself a hideout?"

"Then just the cafeteria."

"Could he be coopting somebody's ID, temporarily like? Just for one meal at a time? I'm figuring he's hacked the personnel system... he seems to be good at that."

"Yeah, I'll look for someone who's double feeding. But what do I do if I find them? Wouldn't he be hopping around from one ID to the next?"

I nodded, "Maybe. Meanwhile, can you find out who the victim's close acquaintances were and get them in here so I can grill them. But I don't want to see anybody till after the autopsy."

"Sure."

"Okay, Mak, it might be nice to debug this room before we get too comfortable. Lijuan, likewise check the local network for eavesdropping viruses. By the way, this goes for everybody, try to keep your communiques private. Don't use the network any more than you absolutely have to. Spoken words are safer than written words. And whispered words are even better. At least they will be when Mak gives us the thumbs up."

Everyone laughed. That was good. Morale was picking up.

"Mak, once we get your blessing on the bug situation, I need you to organize the local security folks into a brute force search of the whole station. I'm guessing our boy may be living in a regular room, but he's keeping his gear somewhere in the bowels of the station. These stations are all cookie cutters of one another, so start with the equivalent location from *Einstein*."

Mak grinned, "Yeah, boss!"

"Oh, and Mak, use extreme caution. Assume the perp has whatever room he's coopted rigged with cameras, microphones, and maybe even explosives. We've been putting pressure on him, so he may be tempted to fire a shot across our bow. Get an engineer to remote probe any suspicious room before you go in. And use a robot to gain access. Got that?"

The grin fell from Mak's face, "Yes, boss."

I settled into my new room on *Borucki* and set up a two-way text conversation with Chief Ciccolella. Since he was Earthside there was a barely perceptible lag in the communications.

Stone: I'm worried about the captain on Borucki. Name: James Nation. He may be more than a nuisance, i.e., he may become a body-count multiplier.

Ciccolella: SpaceCorp HQ grants you full authority to remove any obstacles that get in the way of apprehending the killer.

Stone: Explain 'remove.'

Ciccolella: 'Exercise own volition' is the precise phrase they gave me. I would say that means if Captain Nation is an obstacle, arrest him. If arresting won't work, shoot him.

Stone: One problem with that, Chief. No gun. Confiscated at Edwards per CisLuna policy.

Ciccolella: You have no weapons at all up there???

Stone: Just the widow maker. And my sap,

Ciccolella: Oh, Christ! I'll see if I can get something up to you.

Stone: Thanks. Meanwhile, it might be helpful if you could get word to the Chief of Security up here. Fellow named Rogers. Seems like an all right guy, but I'd like to know he's on my side if it comes to that.

Ciccolella: Does Rogers have any weapons?

Stone: Not that I know of. His guys mainly do routine candy-ass stuff. Looking after passengers, lost and found, etc. They look like ex-football linemen though.

Ciccolella: How do they handle crime?

Stone: Until now there hasn't been much. None that I've seen. Professional bunch as far as I can tell. This serial killer is way off nominal for them. I think that's why Nation is running around with his asshole retainer nut over-torqued.

Ciccolella: Off nominal?

Stone: I'm picking up the lingo up here.

Ciccolella: Anything we can use down here?

Stone: Nothing really colorful yet. I'll keep you posted.

Ciccolella: Okay, it sounds like we're done for now. Repeat: If Nation is an obstacle, remove him.

CHAPTER FIFTEEN

Autopsy room in the morgue of *Borucki*

Melody Marks, flight nurse, age 29, was attractive, blond, and a virgin.

The staff of *Borucki* had deigned not to leave the corpse lay until I had a look at her. I asked if the people who retrieved her body had worn bunny suits. No they had not. I asked if they had worn slippers. No they had not. I did not bother asking if they had worn gloves. The crime scene was fucked, pure and simple.

Instead my first look at her was when she was laid out under a sheet in the morgue. That pissed me off, and not because I was developing a thing for upside-down dead women. No, a major, major peeve of mine—it always has been—is non-professionals fucking with my crime scene before I get there, and that includes moving the body.

I was glad Martin had offered to come along for the autopsy. The flight surgical staff here was really broken up about losing one of their own. Not that I blamed them.

Monica was gowned and gloved, assisting. I was wandering around observing. Mak was taking pictures. Lijuan begged off citing squeamishness, so I put her on rounding up the close acquaintances she'd identified. I was eager to interview them after the autopsy. Who does a 29-year-old virgin have for close acquaintances anyway?

Flight Surgeon Cooper Murdock was born and raised on a cattle ranch in West Texas. Finished college in Austin, then moved to Palo Alto, California for medical school. Did his residency at the VA Hospital. Got picked up by SpaceCorp shortly thereafter.

"How long had you been seeing Flight Nurse Marks?" I thought I'd try to catch him off guard. It sorta worked—he was startled by the insinuation.

"Seeing her? What do you mean?"

I just stared at him.

"I haven't been 'seeing' her, although if I'm to be honest I guess I would have liked to."

"So why didn't you?"

He twirled the wedding band around his finger. "I have a wife Earthside. She's going to be joining me in two months—you're not going to reveal any of this, are you?"

I looked at him for a few seconds. "Let's start over, how long had you been *working* with Nurse Marks?"

He seemed relieved at the new turn in the conversation. "Two years."

"Tell me about her."

"She was professional—"

"Tell me about *her*, not the flight nurse."

He paused, "Well, she kept to herself mostly. No social life. Never went out with anybody that I know of. Went to mass regularly. Couple times a week."

"How do you know that? Did you see her there?"

"Sometimes. I'm Catholic also."

"A *practicing* Catholic?"

"Uh, not really. I guess I mainly went to see Melody. She was intoxicating!"

I stared at him again. "Can you tell me anything about her behavior or whereabouts on the night she was killed?"

"Not really. She and Madeline helped me with an appendectomy. I left. They stayed to settle the patient in. Didn't see her after that."

"Where did you go?"

"I walked up to the observation deck—good place to relax after you get done carving on someone."

Flight Nurse Madeline Klein was an attractive woman, mid-forties, kind of a baritone voice—very sexy that—and a faint European accent.

"How long had you known Melody Marks?"

She smiled. "Ah, Miss Goody-Two-Shoes. A long time, I guess. Four years on the station, four and a half maybe. And another year Earthside—we were in flight training together."

"Tell me about her."

"Nothing to tell really. She was about as lively dead as she was alive. Her big thing was being sweet all the time."

"*Was* she really that sweet?"

"Oh, yes. She was the genuine article."

"Did you like her?"

"She didn't give you much to like, unless you like diabetes. We worked well together. That's about it."

"Why do you think she came up here?"

She chuckled. "I guess that's one area we had in common. She came up here to be closer to heaven. I came up here to be farther from hell."

"Can you tell me anything about her behavior or whereabouts on the night she was killed?"

"Only that she finished her shift the same time I did. We both went to the cafeteria. I stayed to eat and visit with friends. She got a sandwich to go and left."

"You didn't see her after that?"

"Actually, I did. She was leaving the shower area as I was entering."

"Anything unusual about her?"

"No."

"What was she wearing?"

"White bath robe, towel around her head, slippers, toiletries bag under her arm."

"Did you say anything to her?"

"She just smiled. She was in a hurry."

"A hurry?"

"Her hair was wet. She was not comfortable bathing coed."

"Were there any guys in the bathroom when you went in?"

"Two or three."

"Names?"

"I didn't look at them."

I looked at her quizzically.

"I'm not comfortable bathing coed either."

I couldn't help liking her. Tough, on the cynical side, woman-with-a-past, seen-it-all. She reminded me so much of Emily, Earthside. I thanked her and she got up to leave.

"Oh, one more thing."

"Yes?"

"Is that your natural hair color, platinum?"

"Yes."

I gave her my nice-guy smile. "Would you mind dying it some other color?"

"Yes, I would mind."

"Would you do it anyway? Just till we find this guy?"

"You're telling me he likes blonds?"

"Yes."

She stared at me a second, then walked out.

God, I hoped the next time I saw her she would be right side up.

True to form on *Borucki,* the door to the victim's room had not been sealed. It was locked but anybody with the code could have gone in.

The place was neat, not a thing out of place. There was a stationary box and ink pen lying on top of her desk. I opened the box—she'd started a letter. But I couldn't read it, not much of it anyway, because it was in cursive. Have to put Lijuan on that one. This chick had to be the only person in CisLuna that used cursive. Well, maybe two, counting Lijuan. Surely she didn't expect those letters to get home anytime soon. I checked out her laptop. Mak had cracked the password for me—JesusSaves. She had a file for letters. Ah yes, she imaged what she wrote and sent it home that way. A bit of a personal touch. Certainly harder for some machine overseer to read her mail. Clever girl.

I scanned all the surfaces for prints. There were a ton of them. We'd check 'em all out, but I already knew they'd be mostly her prints and a few prints from the goofs that recovered her body. I was doubtful there'd be prints from any other people, and definitely not the prints I was looking for.

There were some religious artifacts and some Christian-themed pictures hanging on the walls. I checked the picture frames to see if there was anything hidden in them. Nothing. Medicine cabinet had some basic makeup and a standard issue analgesic. Hmm... even God's little angels get headaches. I found some hairs between the bed sheets. I tweezed them into an evidence bag even though I knew they'd be hers. Dresser drawers held the usual undergarments, socks, tops, and scrubs. There was one dress folded up neatly. Another funny thing about space stations. Nobody hangs anything up. Everything gets folded and stuck in a drawer. No closets, no hangers. I guess they save volume that way.

I checked the vent by removing the cover and looking inside both directions. You could tell it had been scraped clean from something that filled up the space about a meter back on either side. Beyond that you could see the usual grit and grease that fills up air vents. Yep, the killer had set up his apparatus in the vent. How did he get his apparatus onto *Borucki*? His coffin would have been awfully cramped. Did he ship it by other means? Did he manufacture a new one? Floor boards revealed nothing but empty space between the joists.

So what have I learned about you, Melody Marks... age 29... sugar sweet blond virgin?

"You coulda been a nun, but you decided to be a nurse."

CHAPTER SIXTEEN

The war room

I'd sent Martin back to *Einstein* with the hope that we would not be needing him again. In his seat looking very uncomfortable was Security Chief Rogers.

"Mak, let's start with you. What do you have on the bug situation?"

"We are clean for bugs. But I plan to keep looking—we only just set up house here and this guy may not have had time to set anything up."

"Good work. What about eavesdropping viruses, Lijuan?"

"Found several that match his signature. Also some standard shit for knocking out security cams and another little gem for playing with door codes."

"Hmm... insipid little bastard, isn't he?"

Only got a couple of chuckles out of that one.

"So are the networks clear?"

"They are not. Every time I try to sponge one virus it morphs into another one."

"What can we do? We have to be able to communicate."

"I suggest we remain very guarded in our communications for now."

"Meanwhile," Mak said, "I'm working on a counter-virus. If we can't eliminate his virus, maybe we can get it to tell us where he is."

I was sitting at my desk in my new digs enjoying a Scotch and having an almost real-time video session with Emily. The watering hole here was affectionately called the Billy Bee and the barkeep didn't mind if we walked off with glasses so long as they were filled with product. He'd said most folks were pretty good about returning them. Meanwhile, Emily had sent me a picture of herself as a brunette.

"Does this look silly?"

"Nope. Brunette becomes you."

"Mind telling me why I did this, apart from making my tips go way down?"

"Perp likes blonds. He's racked up three so far."

"But he's 370 thousand klicks away!"

"I know, but... this just takes away one thing that I don't have to worry about. Things are getting pretty tense up here."

"What about Devil? Won't I be safe with him?"

"Devil's pretty ferocious, but no. This perp takes out his victims with CO_2 asphyxiation. Last time I checked, German Shepherds are not immune to that. Where is he now?"

"He's with me. I'm still at Becky's. I told her about Hanna."

I paused a moment.

"Was that necessary?"

"You've been gone a long time. How long can I take advantage of her on the excuse that I'm afraid of the dark?"

"I guess you're right."

"How much longer do you think this will take?"

"I wish I knew. The guy thinks he's a vampire plus he seems to be a shape shifter and a station shifter. Whenever we think we're close, he changes IDs and jumps to a new station."

"Great. I'm married to Professor Van Helsing chasing vampires on the Moon."

We rang off and I was about to shut down and get some rack, when a pop-up appeared on the screen.

IP TRACE: WIFI CONNECTION QUAD
IV, DECK 1, C-WING, BOX 7.

CHAPTER SEVENTEEN

War Room

I showed Mak my pop-up message.

"It worked!" he said.

"What worked?"

"My counter-virus. I just got it up for the first time late last night. You were being eavesdropped from someplace over in Quad IV."

"How precise is this location?"

"We can't tell precisely where the laptop was located, but we can tell precisely which WiFi transceiver it was using."

"So how far away would the laptop have been, say, maximum?"

"Maybe fifty meters, perhaps less. But you can't tell which direction."

"And how do you know it was our boy?"

"I don't. I just know that whoever eavesdropped on your conversation was using that virus."

"So what do we do with this?"

"Well, for starters, I'd say this greatly reduces my door-to-door search space."

I looked at Chief Rogers, "Looks like this is your baby."

"We're on it."

"Oh, Chief, a reminder—knock! If no answer, back away. Get an engineer to remote probe the room and—"

"And use a robot for access. Got it, boss."

Room C105 was less than twenty meters from WiFi Box 7. I arrived at as fast as I could, but riding in on the people mover from Quad II took some time. By the time I showed up there was quite a crowd gathered in the hall.

I noticed they were keeping their distance from Room C105—good. People were taking this case and the killer's lethality seriously.

I walked over to Chief Rogers, "Whatcha got?"

He motioned me over to a monitor that was about twenty meters from the door. A piece of fiber optic cable trailed from the computer setup down to the door. The monitor showed a piece of wire inside the room. It was attached to the door knob and went to the cabinet under the sink passing into the cabinet through a small hole in the cabinet wall.

"Now we know where he's hiding his Christmas presents."

Chief Rogers said, "We've evacuated C-Wing as well as B-Wing and D-Wing in the vicinity of the room."

"Good thinking." I asked Lijuan what she had on the room.

"Vacant."

"So somebody was just squatting there?"

"Looks that way. Fiber optic shows a few personal belongings on the bed. Bed covers are ruffled. Toothbrush in a glass on the sink. Somebody is living here. They're just not there right now."

"Good work."

I turned to the engineer, "What's the best way to get inside without disturbing that wire?"

The engineer said, "The door is nanocellulose. We can just cut a hole in it with a laser. Shouldn't be too hard for somebody to wiggle through."

"Whoa! Nobody is going near that room until that device—whatever it is—is defused. Also, let's keep in mind that we're dealing with a tricky bastard. That cable from the door knob to the cabinet could just be a distraction. The real device might be under the floor boards, and activated by your foot pressure. Or maybe he's rigged a heat sensor. You can't allow yourself to be narrow minded with this guy. So only the robot goes in the room for now, and then only when all the people are well away."

An hour later the robot entered the room through a hole in the door. It was equipped with a drill and carried a fiber optic cable to pass through the hole it was going to drill into the cabinet. I was breathing down the engineer's neck to see what was inside the cabinet. The hole completed, the robot inserted the cable. Inside we found some random cleaning stuff, some extra toilet paper—some folks insisted on paper up here—and the end of the wire wrapped around the sink drain. Nothing else. No explosives, no detonators, no fancy mechanisms. Just a lousy piece of wire going from a door knob to a sink cabinet. A great big 'Fuck you!'

"Okay," I said. "Nobody goes into that room until the robot has drilled holes in every drawer, ceiling panel, air vent shaft, wall panel, and floor panel."

"That could take days, boss," the Chief said.

"I know." And so does the killer.

About then Captain Nation showed up.

"What's the meaning of this?" he asked.

"What's the meaning of what?"

"Why have you displaced thirty of our good citizens while you pursue one of your wild goose chases?"

I took slow breath before I answered. "We found an unregistered room where apparently, someone has taken to squatting. It might be the killer and I'm worried that he may have boobytrapped it."

"Boobytrapped?"

"Yes, a special kind of bomb or incendiary device—"

"—I *know* what a boobytrap is, Mr. Stone."

"Good. Then you can see the need to take precautions."

"I can *see* that I have people with no rooms."

"It's for their safety."

I guess he ran out of ways to piss me off at that point. He just stood there fuming, his nostrils flaring with every breath.

"Well, be quick about it."

Then he turned and stalked off. *Prissy little fuck.*

When I got back to my room I was the kind of beat that comes from waiting for hours for a bomb to go off, only it never does. I'd stuck around for several hours while the dissection of the killer's room took place. I knew we'd come up dry, but mostly I wanted to be sure no one on the team took any short cuts.

I was ready to crash, but I thought I should check my computer one last time before turning in. When I opened it, there was a pop-up waiting for me. No IP TRACE, just a fucking pop-up message.

NICE TRY

Chapter Eighteen

War Room

I showed everyone the "Nice try" pop-up on my computer screen. "Anyone else get one of these little gems?"

Everyone shook their head.

"What's it mean?" Lijuan asked.

"It's his way of laughing at us... well, me anyway. These demented minds are actually proud of their kills and how they elude capture. It's the excitement of the chase. Sometimes they feel a little bored with just killing people in bizarre ways, so they raise the stakes by saying 'catch me if you can.'"

"Well, he's doing pretty well at that," Mak said.

"How so?"

"My counter-virus no longer works."

"At all? No graceful failure? Just gave out altogether?

"Yeah, boss."

"Well, keep trying. We gotta make the perp feel the pressure so he'll make a mistake."

"Lijuan, how's the duplicate ID search going?"

"I think he on to us, boss. I think he's coopting IDs just to eat. Then after he eats or maybe during the meal he goes in and resets that person's cafeteria attendance."

"How do you know that?"

"I don't actually *know* that, but what I'm seeing is him eating in quads that are completely unrelated to the IDs he steals. The ones he's stealing are from people who live or work in different quads."

"How do you know he's eating at all?"

"I had the hostess at each cafeteria keep a manual count. The computer counter keeps coming up shy by one."

"Is there a particular quad he favors?"

"Quad IV. There's two cafeterias there plus a couple of sandwich kiosks near the work areas. He doesn't seem to go for the kiosks—maybe too personal, not enough traffic to hide in."

At that moment Nation barged in and started flaming all over me. I interrupted him in the middle of his tirade.

"Why don't you all wait outside while Captain Nation finishes with his constructive comments."

Nation went on with his tirade demanding results and threatening to have me replaced with someone competent. I did my best not to smile at that one. After another minute of his abuse, I interrupted asking, "Is any of this getting us closer to catching the killer, or is it just making you feel better?"

Nation said nothing, just slowly turned beet red and walked out.

After the captain left, I walked outside. Everybody was hanging around looking down in the mouth. I peeked down the hall at the departing figure of the captain, then smiled at the team, "The captain wants you all to know you're doing noble work!"

As everyone was going back into the war room, I grabbed Rogers by the arm, "Rogers, my man, mind if an old gumshoe tags along on your room-to-room?"

He smiled, "Not at all."

His team consisted of two of his security guards, the engineer with the robot, Lijuan, and now me. They had a pretty good routine down. Lijuan would look up who was supposed to be living in a room and what their work shifts were. Then we'd try to call them. If they answered, we'd explain that we were doing a room-to-room to determine if anybody had moved in to their room while they were away. Most were too busy to come down and open the door for us, so after the robot peeked in and cleared the place of obvious intrusion, we just opened the door ourselves and walked in and looked around. If it looked like that person lived there, for example a gender match on clothes, then we'd just leave. It was kind of boring until we arrived at a vacant room. Then the engineer would drill a hole in the door and poke his fiber optic cable in for a peak. If it was empty, we'd pull out the cable, seal the hole in the door with a shot of space glue—marvelous stuff that—and be on our way.

More for the sake of team morale than anything else, I stuck it out with them all day. I wasn't going to quit until they did. When they finally quit, Lijuan and I headed for a cafeteria for a late bite. She knew of one that specialized in Chinese food. She got some dim sum and a pot of green tea to go. I was going to do the same but the cook recognized me. Lijuan had told him I was from China Town in Manhattan. He was a jolly little man, his face so rotund and plump it was a wonder he could still see. I liked him right off. He made me feel like I was back at the C&L Dumpling House in the Bowery. He insisted I stick around for some kind of flaming duck. I asked him how he got live duck up here on a space station.

"We don't. We just grow part we need in lab. Duck lot happier that way."

"Does it taste like real duck?"

He laughed, "Sometimes!"

CHAPTER NINETEEN

Hallway Outside Stone's Room

I was about to punch in my door code when I heard some kind of racket inside my room. It sounded like somebody banging on something with the palm of their hand. I wondered if it was the killer. I put my ear to the door... yep, definitely somebody inside rearranging things. I decided I'd just wait him out—he had to come out sometime.

Meanwhile, I called Monica. She answered on the first ring. "Come down to my room right away. I think our boy is inside arranging for my early demise."

"On my way."

I leaned against the wall facing the door, my left foot forward and body crouched with a slight forward lean—my action stance. I pulled the widow maker out of my jacket pocket and hid it behind my thigh, safety off, thumb on the button. In my left hand I had my thumb sap with my first two fingers through the leather strap. If this was the killer, whatever was going to happen was going to happen fast.

After what seemed like an hour—probably about ten minutes—I saw the door latch move. Then the door pulled inside making a swoosh sound and a dark blur came at me in a rush, right arm high and brandishing a pry bar. In the milliseconds before the bar landed, I got a good look at the perp's face, but it wasn't Crowne. By reflex I put my left arm up to block the pry bar and snapped my switchblade open. The pain from the blow to my forearm was excruciating—the bastard had scored a direct hit on my ulnar nerve, aka my funny bone. I didn't find it humorous at all. I swept his right arm to the side with my left arm then came back across his face with the sap, catching him on his right cheek bone. Then I lunged with my blade aiming for his lower torso. I felt good penetration, but his left arm stopped it from being a kill thrust. He got in another blow with his pry bar catching me square on the head and putting my lights out.

When I came to I was leaning against the wall and some musclebound dame was slapping me in the face. When I started to snap out of it, the first thing I remembered was the bastard that whacked me. I tried to get up but the dame pushed me back down.

"I gotta get him!"

"Whoa there, Trigger! You may have a concussion. We gotta get you to sick bay."

I struggled but couldn't shake her off—damn, that broad was strong.

"But I'll lose him!"

"Do you even know which way he went?"

I shook my head.

"Did you get a good look at him?"

"Yeah. It's not Crowne."

Monica grabbed her communicator, "I'm calling security to cordon off the room and an environmental mechanic to deal with the CO_2."

I looked at the door barely hanging by one of its hinges.

"What happened to the door?"

"That's where I found you. I think he threw you on the bed and activated his CO_2 mechanism. When I got here the door was locked. You didn't answer when I banged on it, so I dialed your communicator. When I heard it ringing inside the room, I knocked the door in and found you. You were damned lucky. What made you think you could take him by yourself?"

"Well, it's my job for starters. And, I had my widow maker and my sap."

I was still holding my stiletto.

Monica raised her eyebrows and opened her mouth wide.

"What? You knew I carried a blade."

"Yes, but now it has blood on it."

I looked at my hand. "Why so it does! I guess I got a piece of him!"

I reached for a handkerchief to wipe the blade.

"Stop!" She grabbed my arm. "You got a piece of him all right—a piece of his DNA! We can nail whomever we catch if their DNA matches."

I grinned in spite of the pain in my arm and the worse pain in my head. "Yes, we can! Assault, breaking and entering at the very least."

"And assuming we can find his CO_2 apparatus in there, that should be attempted murder."

"Yeah, we just have to catch him."

I struggled to my feet. I was still pretty wobbly but after Monica helped me up I could stand alone. Sort of.

"So it looks like I maybe got two inches of penetration, judging from the blood smear."

"You got him in the torso?"

"Yeah."

"Show me where and what angle."

I put my index finger against her stomach, "About like this."

"Hmm... it probably went through the rectus abdominis and possibly penetrated the transversalis fascia and parietal fascia."

"Translation?"

"There is a slight chance the knife penetrated the small bowel. If it did, the wound is guaranteed to fester and he will likely die without treatment. If not, he may be able to stitch the wound himself. And if that doesn't fester, he will recover."

"So you figure he's heading for his hideout to treat himself?"

"Right. If he turns himself into sick bay he's as good as captured."

"This may be our best chance yet to get this guy. We gotta get the team down here to look for a blood trail."

"And what if they find him?"

"Do not approach. Nobody plays the hero."

"You mean like you did?"

"Okay, I had that coming. New plan. We know he's gonna be holed up somewhere licking his wound. Doubtful he'll be back to recover his gear from this room. Meanwhile, I want that CO_2 apparatus. If we know what it is and how he deploys it, we may be able to fuck up his next kill."

Monica nodded, "Okay, but I think he's going to try to jump ship as soon as possible—he's in no condition to commit another murder, at least for now. And the longer he stays on *Borucki*, the worse his odds of evading capture."

She started leading me down the hall, "You gonna come quietly or do I have to get rough?"

Quietly seemed like the best option so I shuffled along beside her.

"Where we goin'?"

"Sick Bay."

"But what about the blood trail?"

"We'll get Rogers to assemble a team of his blood hounds. Mak and Lijuan can form another team. When one team finds the trail, the other can join them."

"You have a keen tactical mind for a molecular biologist."

"Would you hold my hand so I can get your jacket off?"

The flight nurse was a cute redhead. I shook my head. "I can't feel my fingers."

"That's a really nice jacket. I'd hate to have to cut the sleeve off. Is that real leather?"

I gritted my teeth and pulled the sleeve off with my good hand.

She started to take a scissors to my khaki shirt sleeve.

"Hey, wait, that's the only shirt I have up here."

"We'll get you a coverall."

"No way! Just unbutton the front and I'll wiggle out of it."

My left forearm was bruised and swollen where the pry bar landed.

Then the flight surgeon started shining lights in my eyes and making me look left and right and up and down.

"Detective Stone, you have a concussion. We need to admit you for observation for at least 24 hours."

"I have to get someone on that blood trail."

"I'm sure you do, Detective. But right now you are wobbly, nauseous, and having trouble forming coherent sentences. Plus, the x-ray shows your left ulna has a minor fracture."

The flight surgeon took the phone out of my left hand—I was too weak in that arm to put up a fuss.

"Hey, I need that."

"You *need* a Zip-Kast on that arm and at least twenty-four hours' observation. Monica will help you with your investigation."

"Where the hell is Monica anyway?"

"I think she's preparing a solution to get a blood sample off that knife blade. Where'd you get that thing anyway? It's a beauty!"

"It's Italian. Got it in New York City when I was twelve."

About then Monica walked up with my knife in a plastic bag. The blood smear was gone.

"Did you get your sample?"

"Yup, I'm going to scooter it back to the lab on *Einstein* for DNA sequencing."

"Can I have my knife back now?"

She opened the bag and took the knife out. The blade was still open.

"How do you close this thing anyway?" I took it from her and depressed the backside swivel bolster with my thumb. This released the blade lock so I could close the blade against the side of my leg. Then I slid the safety button back to 'safe' and put the blade in my pocket.

"You must have had an angelic childhood."

I shrugged, "There were very few angels in the Bowery when I was a child."

I got a message from the crew dissecting the evidence in my room. It had a picture of a strange looking apparatus laid out on the floor. I got an incoming call from the fireman.

"Stone here, whatcha got?"

"We had to run a compressor to flush the leftover CO_2 from the room. Then we pulled these two CO_2 bottles out of the vent. There was one on each side. They would have held about 4 kilos each when full. These inflatable bladders they're wrapped in effectively seal the vent. There's some kind of RF device attached to the valves on the bottles."

"Were they full?"

"No empty. If that dark-haired woman hadn't pulled you out when she did, you'd a been a goner."

Monica, you are one beautiful, beautiful musclebound babe. I wondered if I dared say that to her face.

CHAPTER TWENTY

Sick Bay

My communicator vibrated, "Stone here."

"Hey, boss. We think we found the hideout."

"Don't touch the—"

"The door. We know."

"Where's Rogers?"

"We already called him, he's on his way. Probably twenty minutes before he gets here—he's on the other end of the quad."

"Okay, get an—"

"An engineer and fire crew. They're on the way too."

"Okay, I'm going to try to sneak out of this sick bay as soon as Monica gets back from shipping her sample. See you in twenty mikes if I can find my clothes. If I can't, I'll be the guy with his butt sticking out of the paper hospital gown."

I showed up at the hideout riding pillion on a narrow gauge golf cart driven by Monica. Clever little contraptions those.

When they sense a zero-gee situation they harpoon themselves to the deck.

"Whatcha got?" I said to Mak as we pulled up.

"See the engineer with the drill? That's where the blood trail ended up. He should be streaming his FO cable back to us any second now."

I noticed everybody was keeping about thirty meters back, even the fire crew. They were in full panoply with backpack fire extinguishers, full Nomex™, and helmets equipped with face shields. Slung from their waists were small compressed air bottles feeding masks that were hanging open from their helmets. One of them was holding a rope that attached to the engineer. Real pros on this station.

"Good work," I said, then turned to find Lijuan.

"Lijuan, can you check flight schedules?"

"Any particular one you're looking for?"

"Anything leaving *Borucki*. Make me a list of the next week's worth of departures."

I turned back to the fire crew. "Chief, what are your guys doing?"

"We've cleared the entire wing, and I got two-man teams at each end making sure it stays that way."

The engineer walked back from the door paying out his fiber optic cable. We all crowded around as he attached it to his computer. The room was dark but the FO cable was Siamesed to a light cable that acted as a flashlight. There was no wire attached to the doorknob or the sink cabinet. In the middle of the floor was a pair of bladders that looked like deflated water wings. Each was wrapped around what looked like a fire extinguisher bottle, maybe three or four kilos each. It was the same apparatus he used in my room.

Lijuan tugged at my jacket sleeve, "Boss, I got your flight schedules." She showed me her laptop screen and pointed to a single line. The SpaceCorp Moon Shuttle *SMS Anthony Colaprete* was set to leave within the hour, destination Lunar South Pole.

I looked at Lijuan, "You think he could be on it?"

Lijuan flipped the page to a manifest. "While I was checking the passenger list, this name popped up. I think this is our boy. He's going by the name Jonathan Teach now. Station roster has no record of anyone named Teach."

"Monica! We gotta get to the Lunar Shuttle Port ten minutes ago! We're looking for a new passenger addition named Jonathan Teach."

I turned back to Lijuan, "You and Mak stay here and supervise the fire crew. Under no circumstances let the fire crew or anyone else to attempt to open that door!" I climbed into the pillion seat behind Monica on the golf cart.

As we dashed off, I shouted, "Lijuan, get that shuttle flight held!"

CHAPTER TWENTY-ONE

Lunar Shuttle Launch Port

We arrived at the passenger terminal to find it empty except for a few hangers-on who wanted to watch a shuttle departure on the monitors. The shuttle had just been freed from her hold-downs and was speeding away from *Borucki* at 70 meters per second. I grabbed a flight technician, "Is that *Colaprete*?"

He smiled, "Why yes, it is!" He must have read my expression. "Is there a problem?"

I muttered more to myself than to him, "You have no idea..."

Monica smiled at him, "He's just upset because he wanted to watch the departure. He's never seen one from the station before."

"Oh, well you can replay the recording on line."

Monica dragged me away, "Thanks, we'll do that!"

I was feeling weak and a little dizzy from the excitement. I sat down on the pillion seat of the golf cart. The flight technician, bless his heart, followed and began a litany about lunar surface shuttles.

"*SMS Anthony Colaprete* was the first crew shuttle designed to service Colaprete Station, hence, its name. Crew shuttles perform an essential role of swapping out lunar surface crews after a month of surface duty. Prolonged duty on the Moon at one sixth gee causes decalcification of the bones. So, SpaceCorp policy wisely calls for one month of lunar duty to be followed by two months of recuperation on *Borucki*."

I sat and listened while I caught my breath. This information might actually be useful if the perp was planning to set up shop on the Moon.

The flight technician rambled on, "The lunar surface contingent numbers about 300 personnel at the two water works located at the north and south poles, plus a smaller contingent of about a dozen who are out scouting around for minable deposits of Helium-3. Helium-3, if found in rich enough deposits, would be extremely valuable for fusion propulsion. Anyway, providing 600 lunar surface crew with a place to hang out in full gee was the primary function of *Borucki*. A space station only needs about 300 crew to keep her flying and maintained in a relatively low hazard area like Earth-Moon Lagrange Point 1. Hence, they have little difficulty accommodating 600 lunar surface crew awaiting deployment."

I interrupted, "Tell me about the shuttle launch. How's it work?"

The flight tech smiled at the chance to show off his knowledge, "Prior to launch, a shuttle like *Colaprete* would be secured in a horizontal position to the hangar deck floor. At launch the hangar roof will open and the hangar floor will lift the shuttle until it is even with the outer hull of the station. The hull rotates at 1.34 rpm to provide a full gee at the rim giving it a rim speed of 70 meters per second which is used to launch the shuttle tangentially away from the shuttle. A few minutes after release, the shuttle is over the mandatory safe separation of 100 km and can light the nuclear lightbulb engines for a decent trajectory to the lunar surface where it lands in a conventional vertical fashion."

"Wait," I said. "Can they turn around if they haven't lit their nukes yet?"

The tech looked perplexed at my question. "Possibly. I wouldn't really know."

I grabbed Monica's arm, "We have to get to flight ops. Make 'em call that thing back!"

Monica gently took my hand off her arm, "I'll take you to flight ops if you really want to go there, but they can't call that shuttle back. Once it left the hangar, it was committed. It'll be setting down on the lunar surface in about an hour and a half."

She led me over to a couch and laid me down with my feet on her lap. The return of blood to my head cleared my head.

"So now what?" she asked.

I thought a minute, then said, "Can you get that flight tech back over here? See if he'll show you the names on his manifest. We need to confirm Jonathan Teach was on that flight. Then find out if they check off the names of debarking passengers down on the surface."

While Monica was talking to the flight tech, I called Lijuan. "Can you send me a list of upcoming shuttle flights going down to the surface?"

"I'm going to have to call you back on that one—the captain is here ordering his fire crew to force the door."

"Christ on a crutch! Let me talk to him. They need to get a robot to open that door. There could be a bomb—"

There was a loud boom over the comm link. A full minute went by while I waited for Lijuan, wondering if I was ever going to hear her voice again.

"You called that one, boss."

"Monica and I are on the way back. Gimme what you know."

"There was an explosion from the hideout as one of the fire crew attempted to force the door. Captain's orders."

"Casualties?"

"Looks like the fire crewman... Nothing left of him. Maybe a couple of other crewmen. Too much smoke to tell for sure. I think the engineer. All gone."

"What about the captain—was he hurt?"

"No, he was back here with Mak and me and the fire crew chief."

"Good. I was hoping to save that pleasure for myself."

"Get in line. Mak's trying to keep the fire crew chief from killing him."

"Stone!" the captain shouted. "I'm going to have you in irons! Look at the shambles your murderous incompetency has made of my station!"

I ignored him, no mean feat since he was shouting in my ear. I made my way over to Lijuan, "Where's Mak?"

"He's helping the fire crew. What's left of them."

The captain grabbed me by the arm and continued shouting. He'd really lost it. Spit was coming out of his mouth and getting all over my face—something I can't stand. I grabbed his lapel with my good arm and shoved him against the bulkhead, my casted arm across his throat.

"Shut your fucking spaghetti-hole, Captain!" I had my mouth pressed close to the side of his face so my snarl would penetrate all the way to the middle of his pea-brain.

Then I dragged him over to ground zero, stopping when I found a human leg lying on the floor. It had a fireman's boot on the end, the rest of the leg was bare up to the stump just above the knee. I forced the captain down onto his knees to look at it.

"*This* used to be one of your crewmen, *Captain. This* is all that's left of him! *This* is what happens when your people don't follow my instructions because of your goddamned orders! I warned them there would likely be a bomb in there. Goddamn you, you... sanctimonious sonuva bitch! I warned them!"

I guess I didn't realize how rough I was getting with the captain—I practically had his face mashed into the bloody leg. Mak came up and pulled me away from him.

The captain got to his feet and dusted off his tunic. He looked around at the silent faces of the fire and security crew. His voice was cold and stony. The fact that he had finally angered me seemed to calm him.

"Take this man into custody."

Nobody moved.

Then he shouted, "That's an order! Take this man into custody!"

I shook myself free of Mak's grip and approached the security men. Then in my calm voice I said, "As the on-site legal representative of SpaceCorp, I am relieving Captain Nation of his command. Please escort him to his cabin where he shall remain under house arrest until further notice. Post a 24-hour guard outside his door."

One of the security guards let slip a smirk but quickly wiped it off. The guards were big guys. One of them got on each arm of the captain, lifted him up and walked him toward his quarters, his comical feet kicking the air.

"This is mutiny! I can have you executed!"

Mak looked at me, "You better sit down, boss. Before you fall down."

"Just steady me, Mak. I need a look in that room."

A day later, we were gathered in the war room, it being the only place big enough to hold all of us. Hank Larson's head and shoulders were on the big wall monitor while he cross-examined my decision to arrest Captain Nation. Chief Ciccolella was auditing the meeting from a smaller inset on the monitor. Samantha King, captain of *Einstein*, was also conferenced in via another inset on the monitor.

"Where is Captain Nation right now?" Hank Larson asked.

"In his quarters, sir. House arrest," the Chief of Security said.

"Chief Rogers, in your professional opinion was Detective Stone's action necessary?"

"Uh, as someone who was on the scene, I would say it was. Yes, sir. *Very* necessary."

"Who is running the station right now?"

"First Officer Boswell, sir."

"Boswell... where is he right now?"

"Uh, *her*. First Officer Boswell is a woman. She's on the bridge, sir."

"Okay, Sam, can you speak to Detective Stone's competency on this case?"

"Yes, I can. He is more than competent. I'd say bordering on prescient."

"Was his decision justified?"

"I can't speak to that since I wasn't there. I defer to the senior officer on the scene, Security Chief Rogers."

"Rogers? Can you attest to Detective Stone's competency?"

"Yes sir. Detective Stone's orders to leave the door intact for a robot to breach was very sound. Captain Nation's decision to force the door almost resulted in a hull breach and many more lives lost."

"Any idea where the killer got that much high explosive on a space station?"

I jumped in at this point. "It wasn't high explosive, sir. He rigged a fuel-air device, probably got a small supply of LH2 and then rigged something to mist it into the room. Then a tiny spark and you'd get a blast that, as Chief Rogers described, could have resulted in a hull breach. If the perpetrator's hideout had been another deck closer to the outer hull... Well, we were damned lucky."

"Detective Stone, where is the perpetrator now?"

"We believe he is on the Lunar surface."

"Has the Lunar surface commander been notified?"

"He has, but in the excitement he was not so informed until after the shuttle landed and her passengers debarked. I'm told that whereas embarking passengers are carefully screened, the same is not true of debarking passengers."

"Can't they just round up this Teach fellow from their general population?"

"No, sir. No one by the name of Jonathan Teach ever arrived. He boarded the shuttle—we think—but he never got off. He seems to be able to change his identity at will. Probably the finest hacker I've ever seen. Anyway, we don't know what name he's going by right now."

"What steps is the surface commander taking to contain the killer?"

"Nuthin', I hope. I told him to sit tight until we get there. I need the perp to think he got away. For now."

"And when will you get there?"

"I'm hitching a ride in a few days on an LH2 shuttle to reconnoiter. Meanwhile, the regular surface shuttle is going to take my team and some special equipment down a week from now."

"Can't we scramble a shuttle to get you down faster?"

"We could, but that would arouse suspicion. We need him overconfident. We need him to think he got away."

"You have a plan?"

"Yes, sir."

When I didn't elaborate, he grinned and asked, "Do I get to know what it is?"

"All due respects, sir, but I'd rather you did not. Communications up here are less than secure."

"You don't even trust our laser link?"

"I get the idea of a laser link and it sounds really snazzy, but this guy is scary smart. If he wants to, he can crack any system we have. Our best defense is covertness. I'm kinda worried we may have said too much already."

"Have you told anyone else the nature of your plan?"

"My team—Monica, Mak, Lijuan, Rogers. And I gave Captain King a heads-up, but no details."

At the mention of Monica's name, Larson's face brightened.

"Hi, Monica!"

"'Lo, Hank!"

"Are you good on Detective Stone's plan?"

"I am."

"Sam, how about you?"

"I'm cool, sir."

"Then if there is no other business, I suggest we adjourn and let Detective Stone get on with it."

As the room emptied, I heard Hank continuing the conversation with Sam and Chief Rogers, "We need to get Boswell patched in to discuss what to do about Captain Nation. Chief Ciccolella, you stick around too. We need more than a security force on the stations. Twelve stations up there with a thousand-odd people on each one—hell, it's time we had a police force."

"And a legal system, sir." Chief Ciccolella said. "This business of hanging felons from the nearest yard arm is a bit dated."

I heard Hank's laugh as I walked out the door.

Outside, I caught up with Monica. "You know this Hank guy?"

"Yup."

"I never met him before."

"He's good people."

CHAPTER TWENTY-TWO

Crew Cabin of an LH2 Shuttle

Monica helped me get settled into the jump seat on the LH2 shuttle. Like the shuttle I rode up here, LH2 shuttle cockpits are evacuated. I guess they figure with all that LH2 there's no sense adding an oxidizer to the mix. Hangar areas on all stations are also evacuated for the same reason. We figured riding jump seat on an LH2 shuttle was the quietest way to get me down on the surface.

When she was done strapping me in, she put two of her gloved fingers against her facemask and made a kiss with her lips, then pressed them against my facemask, "Don't take this personal—it's just for luck."

I grinned back at her. "It'll be our secret."

Then she left. She was some classy dame.

It had been a week since Teach had escaped on the passenger shuttle. That was a blessing for me, albeit a trifle frustrating. We thought we had captured all his murder apparatus, but I was still worried that devious bastard would think up some new way to off somebody while we were up here screwing around on the station. On the other hand, at least my head was clear. I had also quit seeing double, and had regained most of my balance. The flight surgeon had taken my cast off and injected me with some kind of fancy stimulus hormones to make the break heal faster. I had full and pain-free use of my left arm again. Meanwhile, I had spent several days boning up on lunar surface operations. I figured the more I knew about what they did down there, the better off I'd be to trip up our perp before he found his next victim.

LH2 shuttles are kind of like oceangoing tankers back when Earth had oil that needed ferrying around. They are topped by a cockpit that seats three—a pilot, copilot, and the flight engineer. The flight engineer spot had been obsoleted some years ago by automated flight control software, but they left the seat in just in case. I was the 'just in case' this trip.

Below the cockpit was the gigantic LH2 tank, 100 meters long. It has a zero-loss system so they don't leak gaseous LH2 into the hangar deck. I know, 'gaseous LH2' is an oxymoron, but that's what everybody calls it.

Underneath the LH2 tank—which they also use for shuttle propellant—sit the twin solid core nuclear thermal rockets. Solid cores are old technology, but they work fine for the Moon's one sixth gravity, so SpaceCorp still uses them. Stick the nukes inside a beryllium shadow shield to keep the gamma rays pointed away from you and you're good to go. Well almost. You still need a folding tripod landing gear at the lunar surface.

Takeoff from the station was pretty simple. The whole contraption is lying on its side secured to the hangar deck. When it's time to go, the hangar deck floor is raised flush with the outer hull surface. At the right moment—timing is everything in space travel—the shackles are released and the shuttle flies away on a tangential trajectory away from the station. Once it's about a hundred klicks away they light the rockets for the descent trajectory to the lunar surface.

"Easy peasy lemon squeezy," I said.

The copilot turned around and tapped his mike switch.

"Sorry." Did I just say that with a hot mike?

I would have liked to look out the window to admire the view on the way except that there were no windows. The pilot and copilot shared a giant monitor with lots of graphs and surface plots. They didn't give me anything. Not even a toy steering wheel with a plastic horn that wouldn't work in the vacuum. So, I went over my plan one more time.

Down on the surface, Commander Higgins was going to meet me an hour after touchdown. That would technically be around midnight except that it never gets dark at the lunar south pole. The idea was to give the regular crew a chance to clear the area and convince anyone who was watching that there were no passengers.

Once on the ground, Higgins and I would take the tunnel trolley to a separate barracks used by one of the special 6-man crews that was currently out prospecting for Helium-3. I read that Helium-3 will be important for fusion power someday, if they ever find rich enough ore. The important thing is that the barracks is far enough away from the rest of the water works gang so they can't see what we're up to. Hopefully Teach, or whatever name that asshole was going by now, would not be able to spot me and clop me on the head with his pry bar again.

A few days later, Monica and the rest of the crew are supposed to bring down a small genetic sequencing device. Higgins told me there was a small room off to the side of the mess hall where we could set up our 'screening lab.' Rogers and a few of his men would shunt people from the chow line into the lab for a simple little test. Nothing more than a cotton swab inside the cheek and then you could go eat your meal in peace. Lijuan, dressed up like a flight nurse but with gloves and a face mask, would check badges against a roster of the people as they made their way in to the mess hall.

The story we would circulate was that Human Research had found a genetic linkage between a particular mineral found on the Moon and a rare form of virulent cancer. I was going to say contagious but Monica shot me down on that one. *"Everybody knows cancer is not contagious. Tell them it's curable but only if we get to it in time."* 'Curable if gotten to in time' That works. So anyway, 'SpaceCorp is now ordering all lunar surface crew to undergo genetic screening.'

We anticipated two possible outcomes of this little scam. The first possibility was that Teach would be unaware that we now had his DNA on file and would just go quietly through the genetic screening. Once we had positive ID—maybe fifteen minutes after sampling—we'd just grab him inside the mess hall while he was eating. We set the probability of this outcome at less than ten percent.

The second possible outcome was that he would figure the cancer story was bogus and that we were out to nail him with the DNA we got off my knife. He would then avoid the mess hall and attempt to stow away aboard the next shuttle heading back to *Borucki* since that was the station that housed all lunar surface workers. Mak and a few of Rogers' men were maintaining continuous surveillance on all outgoing shuttles to try to catch anyone sneaking aboard. If that happened I would attempt to board the shuttle and apprehend him. Truth be told, Monica is better suited than me to bring the guy down, but as a civilian deputy I couldn't ask her to do that. This was going to be on me. Besides, if things went sideways in the screening room, we needed somebody there who could handle herself.

It was a good plan. If Teach was on the Moon, we'd either flush him out or starve him out. Yeah, *if* Teach was on the Moon. We are gonna be so fucked if he's not.

PART III

Chapter Twenty-Three

Passenger Area

Landings on the lunar surface are always done in the traditional vertical fashion. There is a large concrete pad— actually a regolith surrogate for concrete—in the bottom of a nearby crater. The crater walls keep detritus from the landing rockets from spattering structures and/or people that don't take well to high velocity debris.

A gantry collected the pilot and copilot as soon as the hatch opened. I bided my time after they left with my suit plugged in to the umbilical for O2 and heat. They rode the gantry down to a tunnel system that is evacuated for the first hundred meters. Then they went through an airlock and entered a passenger area much like the ones on the space stations. At that point they could remove their helmets and gloves. There are no suit lockers at the surface colonies. People can be miles away from the passenger area and suits are best kept nearby should there be an impact or other form of structural breach.

An hour after the regular pilot and copilot left, the gantry returned for me. On it was the lunar surface commander, Henry Higgins. He seemed like a likeable chap from what I could tell through his helmet visor.

"May I call you Henry?" I asked.

"Hank, please," he answered a little too quickly.

I wondered why he didn't like Henry.

"Okay, Hank it is. Call me Roy."

We shook hands with our gloves on.

"You mentioned you wanted to get out of sight as soon as you got here. Let's collect your things and load them on the golf cart, and I'll drive you out to the hooch where you will be staying until the rest of your team gets here."

He drove the cart over to an airlock and said, "How's your air holding up?"

I checked my O2 bottles and they were full since I'd been on the cabin umbilical. As soon as I unplugged, my suit began having a hard time keeping up with the chill. I started looking for buttons to push to warm it up a bit.

"This ride going to be very long? It's kind of chilly."

"We're only going half a klick."

Easy for him to say. His suit was designed for lunar surface excursions, a truck compared to my sports car.

"Can you tell me about your operation down here?" I asked between chattering teeth. "It might help me figure out how to flush this guy out, assuming he's down here."

Higgins turned and looked at me chuckling, "You serious?"

"Yeah, gimme both barrels."

"Okay, you asked for it. The Moon's spin axis is only 1.5° off the vertical from its orbital plane. Contrast that with the Earth's 23.5° spin axis and it is easy to see why there are numerous craters at the Moon's poles that are in permanent shadow. Without any atmosphere, water trapped in those craters remains at 25-35 kelvins which is pretty close to absolute zero. Water ice that is trapped here isn't going anywhere any time soon. Over the years quite a lot of this water ice has accumulated, 600 million tonnes at the lunar north pole and a slightly lesser amount here at the south pole.

"It takes about 10 km per second of Delta V—you know about Delta V?"

"Yeah, change in velocity, like a speedometer for rockets."

"Close enough. Anyway, it takes 10 km per second for a rocket to get from the Earth's surface up to LEO and another 3 km per second to get to the Moon. Conversely, it only takes 3 km per second to get from the Moon's surface up to Lagrange Point 1. That 10 km per second savings in Delta V is why SpaceCorp set up a 'water works' at each of the lunar poles.

"The water works run off nuclear thermal generators to convert water ice into its constituent LOX and LH2 by electrolysis. Of the two, LH2 is more important because while nuclear thermal rockets don't need oxidizers, they do need copious amounts of propellant or LH2. The dozen space stations at Lagrange Point 1 only need to do a limited number of burns each year to maintain position. But the Mars rocket being constructed at Lagrange Point 2 is anticipated to need 334 thousand tonnes of LH2, including a 32% propellant margin, for a 93-day roundtrip mission with a 33-day outbound leg, a 17-day orbit, and a 43-day return leg. One LH2 propellant shuttle can carry 2,224 tonnes of LH2, requiring 150 runs to fill the Mars rocket's cavernous hub."

He squirmed around to see how I was doing next to him on the golf cart. "You okay?"

"Yeah," I lied. I was beginning to think I was going to be a copsicle by the time we got to the goddamned hooch.

Higgins rambled on oblivious of my state of frozen torpidity. "Personally, I've only gotten occasional glimpses of the Mars rocket. She's named SpaceCorp Interplanetary Spaceship *SIS Pascal Lee* after some scientist at SETI—did a lot of Mars work."

"How much longer?" I asked.

"Couple minutes. Anyway, *Pascal Lee's* central hub is 800 meters long, nearly as long as the Burj Khalifa in Dubai is tall. There are two spokes mounted amid ships that give her a diameter of 500 meters. She has to rotate at 1.89 rpm to give the crew a full gee at the end of the spokes. We're all wondering if that kind of rpm is going to give the crew the willies from the Coriolis effect. You don't really notice the 1.34 rpm on a station, so who knows?"

"Anyway, *Pascal Lee's* supposed to carry four landers, two manned by humans and two manned by AIs. She'll be looking for life hoping to find something based on DNA, a Second Genesis so to speak. If she can find DNA-based life, there is a promise of incredible riches to be found in genes never before seen in earthbound life. It's analogous to biologists and chemists going into the Amazon rain forest back before it became the Amazon Desert in order to look for new venoms and weird chemicals for the pharmaceutical industry. I read somewhere that used to be a big deal back before genetics replaced chemicals in medical treatments."

We finally arrived at the hooch and I secretly prayed they had the heat on. I was so numb I could barely move myself off the golf cart.

"Helium-3 Team Four is out in the boonies and not expected back for two weeks. You and your team should be good using their quarters. There's plenty of food and water and O2 inside. You can get out of your suit and clean up from your flight."

He shepherded me through an airlock that had air hoses and vacuums to blow all the regolith off our suits and suck it into the vacuum system. Bringing unnecessary regolith indoors is considered very bad etiquette down here, not to mention rough on your lungs after a day or two. Inside the hooch it was delightfully warm and there were noisy air filters going full blast.

"Those things stay on all the time?" I asked.

"There are dust sensors that turn them on automatically to keep the dust under control. No matter how good a job you do in the air lock, you always manage to bring some dust inside. They'll quiet down in a few minutes."

"Great, I'd also like you to stick around for a bit so I can fill you in on the details of this sting operation. There's a lot I didn't want to share over the laser link."

"I was hoping you'd say something like that!"

CHAPTER TWENTY-FOUR

Lunar Landing Site—South Pole

Personnel shuttles landing on the moon are not greeted the way airliners are on Earth. Nobody down here is waiting for a returning loved one or a grandchild coming to stay for the summer. Passengers are just workers down here for a one-month shift. And because the shuttle will not take off again for several days while it's checked out and fueled for a space flight, there is no one waiting to board.

My team consisted of Monica, Mak, Lijuan, and Rogers plus two of his biggest and baddest security apes. They knew they'd be keeping their suits on. After checking to be sure everyone had full O2, I ushered them through the external air lock where I had a pair of four-passenger golf carts waiting.

We made the 500-meter trip to the hooch in about ten minutes. Golf carts aren't very fast. Still everyone was glad to step into the warmth of the hooch.

"They call this a hooch?" Mak asked.

"Yeah, that's their name for any external structure that's not dug out of solid rock."

Essentially, a hooch was a series of carbon fiber arches built on top of a regolith cement platform. The platform was laced with a network of tubes that carried hot air. You could walk barefoot on the floor and it was pleasantly toasty. The structure was covered over with a two-meter thick layer of regolith sand bags. The sand bags were primarily for radiation protection but they also provided limited ballistic protection from micrometeoroids. Close inspection showed that our hooch had sustained a few such strikes. Inside the hooch was about twenty meters long by ten meters wide and about 5 meters high at the peak. The actual walking space was only about 5 meters wide since walls had been put up to give the sensation of a rectangular structure. The spaces behind the inner and outer walls were used for O2 and H2O storage, air filtration, and waste treatment. About fifty meters away was a minihooch used for plutonium thermoelectric generators. The triple-redundant cable connecting us to it was covered over with a meter of sand bags as a ballistic shield.

Inside of the hooch were partitioned 'bedrooms,' each with two bunkbeds and a chest of drawers for each occupant. We were careful not to disturb the chests since they were filled with the belongings of the regular crew that lived here. There was a single shower, commode, and sink. The kitchenette was flanked by a picnic-style table that seated eight. There was a lounge area with a big screen monitor for movies or whatever. It had a big couch and three easy chairs. The couch and chairs didn't need a lot of padding given the one-sixth gee down here. Finally, there was an exercise area equipped with spring-loaded exercise contraptions presumably to put maximum weight stress on bones. The hooch seemed over-cozy for a team that intended to spend most of its one-month shift in the boonies looking for Helium-3. Hopefully it would be over-cozy for us too. I was hoping to have our stay wrapped up in a few days.

I added one little gadget missing from all the tech toys found in the hooch—a CO_2 detector.

I had a map of the main facility drawn on a marker board. Like all marker boards that were any good, this one connected to my computer plus it allowed me to draw on it with various colored styluses.

I pulled up a detailed map of the mess area. It was fed by a long corridor that emptied into a 'mud room.' Crew working at the water works spent most of their day suited. Hence, when they came in they needed to go through a pair of water and air showers to get the regolith particles off their suits. The air shower also served as a dryer. Regolith particles are a major pain in the ass down here. The damned things got into everything. Air filtration was a huge maintenance headache. On the plus side, it meant our little scam might be believable. Particles ingested into the lungs—a common occurrence—could cause a persistent cough and over time do permanent damage to your lungs.

Once you were through the mud room and inside the mess hall, you made a right turn to get to the chow line. After your tray was filled, you carried it into the mess hall proper to find a seat and eat your food—all this with your suit on and helmet and gloves off.

We planned to set up a barricade of tables to funnel incoming surface crew through Monica and Lijuan's DNA check station. Monica would do the swabbing and testing, Lijuan was mainly there to check IDs. Rogers had his two guys at the far end of the corridor in case somebody decided to cut and run. Mak and Rogers were to keep an eye on anybody making a break for the shuttles. Mak had the extra duty of monitoring flight manifests to see if any names were mysteriously being added at the last minute. I got myself a lunar surface space suit so I wouldn't stand out, but also so I could roam around outside and give chase to anybody that needed chasing.

Once the team was on the surface I had arranged to curtail any further inbound shuttle traffic until we were satisfied that our boy was found or simply not here. The shuttle that brought us down was being outfitted for a return trip in a week. We left the shuttle in place, the better to monitor anybody trying to surreptitiously book a seat.

"Okay, if there are no questions, let's turn in early. We start this rodeo with the 0600 breakfast meal. Meals are served breakfast, lunch, and supper for three 8-hour shifts. We're going to work through the full three shifts in order to test every crew member down here."

"What if we don't catch him? What's the next step?"

"Lijuan will compare notes with Commander Higgin's staff to see if we got everybody. If someone decided to skip a meal, we go round them up. If that doesn't get him, then we do a modified brute force search where we bring every work team into the mess hall one by one. Once inside, we will have everyone get a good look at everyone else and recite what they know of that person—how long they've worked with him or her, *et cetera*."

"And the helium teams?"

"I've arranged to have them tested as they come in from the boonies."

I looked around the room. Everyone had their game face on—that was good. We all wanted to bag the killer once and for all.

"Okay, let's hit the rack. Wakeup is at 0400. We start testing the mess hall staff at 0530 and their first customers at 0600."

Monica said, "Cool, we might even get to see a sunrise on the Moon!"

Chapter Twenty-Five

Makeshift Lab Next to the Cafeteria

To Monica's great disappointment we did not get to see a sunrise on the Moon. We were at the western end of Cabeus Crater which happens to be in permanent shadow—sorry, Monica. But what it lacked in sunrises, it made up for with gobs of water ice—an ideal spot for a water works.

The mess hall, however, exceeded all expectations with some of the best coffee I've ever had—something about how they had to force feed it through the grounds due to the low gravity. I grabbed the traditional astronaut's steak and eggs breakfast, low bulk, high density, shipped down from *Borucki's* bio-livestock and -poultry generators. I did not want my morning constitutional taking me out of action.

I hung around the mess hall until the first twenty or so surface workers went through the DNA station. They all took it in stride as Monica swabbed the inside of their mouths with cotton swabs. She signaled me over.

"'Sup?" I whispered.

"This would go faster if I had an assistant to work the machine while I take swabs."

"Let me talk to Higgins. Maybe he's got an off-duty corpsman."

An hour later she had a corpsman but no customers. Mess hall staff was busy cleaning up and getting ready for lunch. I went over to the corpsman, "We're going to need you for three shifts. You up for it?"

He shrugged, "Sure, why not?"

"Much obliged."

"Mind if I ask what this is all about?"

"Cancer screening. Certain genomes are susceptible to elements in the regolith. It's pretty nasty unless we catch it early and pull them out of rotation."

I went back over to Monica who was busy with her machine. "I'm gonna go see how Mak is doing with his manifests."

"Yeah," she said not looking up.

Because of her tone I asked, "You got something?"

This time she stopped and looked at me, smiling sort of, and said, "Go see Mak. I'll call you if something comes up."

Mak was up in flight ops, suited but with his helmet and gloves setting on the table beside his monitor.

He had the place to himself. The flight guy that let him in had skipped out for breakfast a half-hour ago since there was no incoming or outgoing traffic scheduled for that day.

"How's it going?" I asked.

"Peachy, boss."

I noticed he had a cup of coffee and a half-eaten doughnut beside his computer.

"Talk to me. Whatcha got here?"

"Just a manifest with thirty names on it. I made a printout so I could see in realtime if somebody new shows up. The way this guy covers his tracks, this might be the only clue I get. I just need to not go crazy for the next twenty-odd hours."

"Maybe I could get Rogers to spell you after a bit?"

"Thanks, but let's keep the muscle where it will do the most good."

I patted his shoulder, "You're doing noble work."

He chuckled, no doubt recalling the last time I'd used that phrase on him.

"Keep it up, pal. I'm hoping once he gets wind of the scam in the mess hall, he'll make his move to get off this rock."

Back at the hooch, the team, including myself and Higgins and a couple of people we had drafted from his crew, had all been at it for 24 hours, taking time out for the occasional potty break and little else. We were beat.

I looked at Higgins, "This guy is scary smart. He must have gotten wind of what we were up to and gone to ground."

"You mean if he's here at all," Higgins said.

I felt myself blush, "Yeah, there is that possibility. If so, then I apologize for the inconvenience we put you through."

"No apology needed, Roy. The last thing I want down here is to find one of my people upside down and no blood. The crews on *Borucki* and *Einstein* must be scared shitless."

"Well, the blond females are. Anyway, I'd like to try one more thing before we pack up and head back to *Einstein*."

"Okay, I'm game."

"It's a kind of brute force search. Rogers' guys and some of your guys will go room to room trying to find somebody we overlooked from the DNA scan. While they're doing that, I want to cram everybody into the mess hall that we can, segregated by work group. Everyone will have their helmets off and give everyone in their work group a close inspection and describe all his workmates in terms of name, how long he's known him, and any other pertinent details he can think of. Lijuan will audit the process to ensure we got each member of the team during the DNA scan. Monica will be on hand to retest anyone who looks suspicious."

Higgins wrinkled his brows, "How's that supposed to find the killer?"

"The perp is a master of disguises. He can 3D print a face of anyone he has a picture of. What he can't print is detailed anecdotal information that you can only pick up working with a team."

"So you think he may have murdered one of my people and stashed the body somewhere?"

"I hope not, but yeah, that's possible."

Everybody was tired and the yawns were getting infectious.

"Why don't you all turn in? I need to discuss a few possibilities with Rogers and the Commander."

It took less than five minutes for everyone to be in their racks.

"Okay," I said when everyone had gone, "how much control do you maintain over golf carts or other conveyances that might be used to get to another hideout at another water works?"

"We don't control golf carts. There's about a dozen of them, but they lack the range to go more than a few kilometers before needing to juice up again. They have RFIDs in case somebody needs to grab one. We have some larger vehicles—lunamogs—that carry ten passengers plus a two-man driver team. They can also pull an equipment trailer. They're used by the helium guys mostly, but we have three more back here as spares."

"And you told me the helium crews all deployed before *Colaprete* landed?"

"That's right. And there have been no landings since."

"Is it possible he never got on *Colaprete*?" Higgins asked.

"You mean he put his name on the manifest as a red herring?" I looked upward rubbing my eyes and sighed, "Yeah, that's possible."

"Do you think he could have grabbed a lunamog and skipped out to the boonies on his own?"

I nodded.

"What, you think he might be hiding out in a cave somewhere waiting for you and your team to get bored and go home?"

I nodded again.

"That's easy enough to check out. We can check the lunamogs to see if any are missing. We can also get a headcount from each of the helium teams to see if they have any new guys."

I shook my head, "he could be wearing a mask he made from one of the crew—long shot. But the best way to tell for sure is to call them in one by one and ID them by DNA."

"Or send you guys out to rendezvous with the helium teams one by one. How many of those DNA sequencers do you have?"

"Just the one."

"Okay, it's late. Let's turn in and revisit this idea after tomorrow's search."

CHAPTER TWENTY-SIX

The Mess Hall

I let the team sleep in until the first shift lunch meal. They needed the rest and I needed them sharp.

Each shift ate by work crew. And as it turned out, there were six work crews numbering between six and ten people, and twenty-six individuals working solo positions. Mostly the shifts were down for three meals per day, but I was told it was common for someone to come in for a sandwich between the two off shifts. That meant this technique wasn't going to be completely leak proof, but it would be pretty tight.

I had each group gather in a circle with their helmets off. Then I'd scan each face with the video on my communicator, pausing at each face so they could say their name and date and place of birth. If I needed to recheck a work crew, I could line them up again and check the count with my video record. The crews were cooperative. Word had gotten out about the murders and they didn't like the idea of losing a team member to some psychopath any more than I did. I asked

Higgins if this was going to put a crimp in his production schedule. He said yes.

"You don't seem all that bothered."

He showed me a text from Hank Larson, 'Do whatever absurd thing Detective Stone asks for as long as he asks it. Set aside production quotas until he leaves.'

"These production quotas—they gonna be hard to make up?"

"They're just quotas. Set by some suit in an Earthside business office."

"What are they for then?"

"Somebody needed a number to establish how big an operation we needed down here. So they came up with a daily quota."

"How do you know that's enough?"

"We send LH2 shuttles topside and the CisLuna stations get first dibs. The excess goes to the space port at Lagrange point 2 where it's used to fill the Mars rocket. We also try to keep up with the production of disks on the hub. So far we can fill them faster than they can build them."

SpaceCorp was sounding more and more like the Army all the time.

This day was long but shorter than yesterday. We finished the last of our face-to-face searches by breakfast of the third shift. I audited the show-and-tell presentations—I didn't get them all, but I got most of them.

Unless Rogers turns up something, this wily bastard will have given us the slip once again.

Rogers showed up after breakfast of the third shift. I could tell from his expression that he came up dry, but I asked him anyway.

"Any luck?"

"Nothin'."

Mak came down from flight ops for some coffee.

"How's the manifest modification business?" I asked.

He showed me his tablet. "*Colaprete* is supposed to depart in three days and the same thirty names are on it."

"What about the LH2 shuttles?" They had been held up while production was halted.

"Nothing there either. The same crew members were kicking back in the pilot hooch. We surprised them with an onsite DNA visit in between breakfast and lunch the same day we did the rest of the surface crew."

It was becoming intuitively obvious to the casual observer that the son-of-bitch was never here.

CHAPTER TWENTY-SEVEN

Albert's Bar, *SSS Albert Einstein*

"You guys seem kinda quiet. Mind if I join you?" Joe asked brandishing a fresh bottle of Scotch.

Sam looked at me and I looked at the bottle.

"That a single malt?"

"Of course."

"I guess we can be bribed," I said as I pulled a chair out.

After Joe serviced all the glasses, he rapped his knuckles in a short riff on the table top. "So, what's the haps?"

"'The haps?' Man, I haven't heard that expression since... shit, not since I was maybe ten years old!"

Joe blushed a little, "Been reading an old mystery novel. Thought I'd pull it out of mothballs, see if it still floats."

The table went back to being quiet again.

"Should I put some music on? What I gotta do to liven this party up?"

"Find me some new leads so I don't have to go back Earthside tomorrow?"

"Sorry. But, hey! You probably put the fear of Satan in his pants. Bet he snuck onto the first shuttle he could find to get back to Earth! That possible?"

Monica jumped in, "Actually, Joe, the favorite theory is that the knife wound he got from Roy perforated his bowel and he crawled off to die a miserable death somewhere."

"Yeah, I heard about that. A switchblade! That was some kinda action, Roy!"

I tilted my head toward him to show him my scar from the pry bar.

"It coulda gone either way. If Monica hadn't shown up when she did—"

"You got it on you?"

"What, my blade?"

"Yeah, I've never seen one except in really old movies. That's the really cool thing about being up here. The movies and all. They don't make 'em anymore Earthside."

He was right. The Hollywood studios had all been bought out by Bollywood. And that killed the American market since Bollywood couldn't see fit to service a market of only 600 million. I pulled my knife out and flicked the blade open.

"Which movies had switchblade scenes?"

"Couple. *Chinatown*. My favorite scene was that one from *Prizzi's Honor*."

"Oh yeah, Jack Nicholson! He throws it when she tries to shoot him."

"Yeah, skewers her to the wall."

"Okay!" Monica said, "Time for a new subject."

We all laughed.

"Can you do that?" Joe asked.

"Do what?"

"Throw it."

I looked at him evenly. "Nah, not very well. It's mostly a close-in weapon, faster on the draw than a revolver. I use a .357 for anything beyond arm's reach. That is until the weapons clerk at Edwards confiscated it." I leaned my forehead toward Sam and raised my eyebrows.

"Don't you go lookin' snaky-eyes at me! I don't want no damn guns on my station!"

"Yeah, well, if I'd had my Smith, we'd have our murderer either dead or in custody by now."

"Smith?" Joe asked.

"Smith & Wesson, my snub-nosed revolver."

"Why a revolver? Seems kinda old-fashioned. I woulda figured you for a Glock or something."

"Not when I'm in a hurry. With my revolver, I just pull the trigger and it fires in double action—one step. Doesn't need a safety to fuss with. The ten-pound trigger pull *is* the safety. I tried a Glock once. Never could bring myself to trust their so-called 'Safe Action Trigger.' Your instinct in a situation is to immediately put your finger on the trigger. With a Glock, that's as good as firing the weapon. So I never carried it with a round in the chamber. Had to pull the slide back before I could shoot. Slow, noisy. Two steps to get a round off. Anyway, I could have had that perp, if I'd had my Smith."

"You just said your blade was better for the close in stuff," Monica said.

"Yeah, normally. But he still got away." Monica might have been intrigued with the gun-talk, but the captain was getting bored. I shrugged. "Nah, you're right. I guess I just miss my piece... I feel kinda vulnerable without it." I suddenly realized that Chick hadn't come through on his attempt to get me a firearm up here. That realizations gave me a chill. I tossed back the last of my Scotch. "Is it hot in here?"

Our little party broke up shortly after that. Sam and Monica went off to their respective cabins. Joe offered me another Scotch. I considered it but declined. I still felt a faint buzz from the shot I'd just had. I don't mind a little buzz. Hell, if I did, I'd never drink at all. But, well, you just never knew.

A month had gone by with no new murders. The killer was presumed dead, body not found, case closed pending further developments.

I was about to get on an interstation shuttle that would take me to *Borucki*, the main travel hub up here in CisLuna. If you were going to the Moon, you caught your shuttle at *Borucki*. If you were going back to LEO, you caught another kind of shuttle that spent its life going to and from CisLuna and LEO. The only flights from LEO to Earthside were like the unscheduled one I'd come up here in, *SLS John Marmie*. Normally, LEO shuttles only fly from Earth to LEO and back again. But the extra LH2 propellant they carry to maneuver around LEO can just as easily be applied to continuing on to CisLuna in a pinch. They carry enough internal LH2 to manage the deceleration needed for docking at whatever station they're aiming at. All in all, I was looking at about a week's transit time. Connections are scheduled to get the most payload for a load of propellant, not for individual passenger convenience.

I'd already said my good-byes to Mak and Lijuan. Sam was tied up in some kind of captain's meeting, so she said. I think the real reason was that she was tired of hearing my endless theories of why the killer was still alive and waiting for me to leave so he could pick up where he left off.

Meanwhile, big beautiful musclebound Monica, bless her heart, was there in person to see me off. At least that's what I preferred to think. The real reason was probably that Sam ordered her to make sure I got on that shuttle and off *Einstein*. That theory also tracked with Rogers meeting me in person on *Borucki*. He was supposed to be my escort for six hours while I was waiting for my LEO shuttle. I smiled at Monica.

"You don't suppose—" I was interrupted by the announcer calling for boarding. I gave her one last hopeful look.

"Go home, Roy. Make love to your wife."

PART IV

CHAPTER TWENTY-EIGHT

Passenger Terminal at Edwards

We touched down at Edwards at 1105 hrs., almost a week exactly since I'd departed *Einstein*. I'd been gone over three months. Monica had given me sound advice. It would be good to get home to Emily.

The space suit technician told me the suit belonged to me now. He had a bunch of forms for me to fill out so I could pick it up next trip to space. Meanwhile, it would go in for refurbishment and cleaning—good to go in about three days. Fine by me, but I didn't think I'd been that hard on it. I'd soiled it a bunch of times, but the diaper worked flawlessly so there was no odor or stains. I guess the refurbishing part made sense. You didn't want those things to fail when you're three hours from Earth and three hours from CisLuna.

That part of my arrival went pretty smoothly. The next part, picking up my sidearm from the weapons locker, did not. It seems the clerk in charge of the weapons locker only believed in working an eight-hour day and would not be back until tomorrow at 0800. I wasn't about to hang around all night waiting for him. Besides I had a snub nose .38 that I kept at home as a spare. It would do for a few days until I got a chance to retrieve my .357.

Meanwhile, a crew chief from a chopper informed me that that they were ready for take-off as soon as I got on board.

Good old Chick! If I could have found a car at all, driving would have taken me five or six hours to get home.

The chopper blades were spinning as I boarded. The crew chief politely shoved me inside and made sure my harness was fastened before fastening his own.

I got out my communicator to text Emily. Chick had arranged for the chopper to drop me off at police headquarters where I could pick up a squad car and drive myself home. I told her I expected to be home between 1:30 and 2 a.m. I waited a moment but got no answer.

I put my communicator away figuring she was probably asleep.

I walked into police headquarters and was met by the desk sergeant, another transplanted New Yorker named Lynch— good name for a cop. Lynch knew exactly what I wanted and shoved me an envelope with a set of keys in it.

"Take your time getting the cruiser back to us."

I said thanks and went outside to find the squad car. It was an electric, but it had a full charge. There was a bottle of single malt on the passenger seat. I opened the note. It was from Chick.

"Nice work! See you Monday."

Monday. I had to look at my communicator to see what day it was. It was barely Wednesday. No problem. Even if I slept all day today, that still left me four days to goof off.

As I pulled into our driveway, I noticed the lights were on. Maybe Emily got my message after all. Better be quiet just in case.

Chapter Twenty-Nine

Living Room

When I walked in my front door the first thing I saw was Emily. Her nude body was hanging upside down from the ceiling. I just stood there looking at her.

She had duct tape across her mouth and her hands were secured behind her back with surgical tubing. I couldn't tell if she was alive or dead, or just unconscious. She had dyed her hair back to blond, but the ends of it were dipping into a bloody pool underneath her. She had a neck wound that was still bleeding down the side of her face.

I looked around the room and saw Devil lying in a heap beside the easy chair. His body was very still and there was a red mark where his blood had soaked into the carpet. Then I felt a thump above my right ear.

I woke up when I felt Emily kicking next to me. I was kneeling next to her with my face against her. I don't know how much time had gone by. I had to fight to maintain consciousness. I managed to rise up on all fours.

The duct tape was gone from Emily's mouth, and when she saw me, she started screaming, "Roy, don't!"

She was wiggling violently causing the blood to spurt from her neck wounds. I tried to tell her to hold still but I couldn't talk because of some obstruction in my mouth. I tried to feel what it was and pricked my finger on something sharp that was sticking out of my mouth.

I struggled to my feet to go over to a mirror we have hanging in the living room. Fangs! I tried to pry them out but they were stuck fast. My face and shirt were covered with blood and my mouth had a weird taste in it.

I wobbled back to Emily who was still kicking. I didn't know how much blood she'd lost and I was worried that what little she might have left she needed for her brain. If I cut her down her remaining blood might rush back into her torso and legs and she'd die immediately. In a do-something-even-if-it's-wrong panic I reached for my knife but it was gone. I pulled the phone from my pocket and called 911. The operator answered but I couldn't speak clearly with the damned fangs in my mouth. I tried anyway. I knew protocol required them to dispatch a squad car and a paramedic van as a precaution, so I hung up and texted Ciccolella to come to my house ASAP. I took a picture of Emily and texted that to him. Then I took a selfie of my bloody face and shirt and texted that as well. Hopefully, he'd figure it out.

I went back to Emily who was now unconscious. She was still losing blood from her neck wound so I tried putting pressure on it with my fingertips. But then I worried that the pressure would stop vital blood flow to her head. Her eyes came open briefly and she looked at me. I shook my head and tried to mouth the words, 'Not me! I didn't do this!' Then her eyes closed again. I tried to get a pulse from her wrist. I thought I might have gotten a faint one, but I wasn't sure. I knelt by her side and tried to cradle her head in my arms.

Some minutes later two cops and a couple of paramedics banged on the front door. I ran over to let them in. The paramedics rushed over to Emily, then stopped, frozen by the absurdity of the scene before them. The cops suffered no such hesitancy. They tackled me and wrestled me facedown onto the floor. I felt a heavy knee between my shoulder blades as my hands were cuffed behind me.

I struggled a bit because I wanted to see what was happening to Emily. I wasn't even sure she was alive at that point. From what I could tell they had cut her down. I heard one of them yelling for an IV and saline solution. Somebody wheeled a gurney past me. Shortly after that the gurney went back outside. Eventually I heard an engine rev and a siren trailing off into the distance.

Ciccolella must have showed up before the paramedics took off with Emily. He seemed to know what her state was.

He took one look at me and his mouth dropped open, "What the fuck?"

I tried to talk but he could see I couldn't form intelligible words because of the goddamned fangs. He tried to pry them out with his fingers, but they wouldn't budge. Whatever held them in was strong stuff.

By then forensics was here. Chick asked the guy if he could get the fangs out of my mouth. The poor guy seemed confused about not wanting to disturb the evidence, namely my mouth, and wanting to get me to talk.

Chick told him, "Look, you're gonna lose valuable evidence if you don't get those things out of his mouth. Can't you clip off the fangs and bag them for later?"

The guy ran off. He came back with a pair of dikes having raided my toolbox in the garage. I held still while he clipped them off. At least I was relieved of that damn overbite. I still couldn't close my mouth properly because of the plastic bridge that was still stuck in there. But at least my words were somewhat intelligible.

Ciccolella's phone rang and he walked away to answer it. When he came back his face was very grim.

"Emily?" I asked.

He shook his head and put his hand on my shoulder. "I'm sorry, Roy."

I started sobbing and rolled over onto my side. A few minutes later, the forensics guy came over with some contraption that had plastic tubing sticking out of it.

"I want to suck out the contents of your stomach," he said to me.

"What for?" Chick asked.

"The woman's blood may be in his stomach."

"What! You think I sucked my wife's blood? Bullshit!"

Chick held me down while the forensics guy started ramming the tube down my throat. It had some kind of numbing agent on it to reduce my gag reflex.

He kept saying, "Try to relax and keep swallowing."

I did the best I could to swallow but I was anything but relaxed. A moment later I could see blood filling up a plastic bag attached to the machine.

After they got the tube out of my throat, a cop came over with a 9mm automatic that had a silencer attached to it. He was holding it with a shoelace that he had passed through the trigger guard. The guy showed it to Chick.

"I found it lying on top of the dog's body."

Chick looked at him, "That the one that went missing from the evidence locker last week?"

The guy shrugged.

Chick sighed, "Dust the pistol for prints and bag the suspect's hands."

Then he turned back to me. He looked apologetic for a brief moment, then his face turned stony. "I'm sorry, Roy. I've no choice but to arrest you under Sierra Penal Code Section 187, murder."

Then he turned to a nearby police officer. "Read him his rights and book him." Then in a louder voice to the whole room, "All right, people! Let's clear the area. This is a crime scene. All non-essential personnel outside."

Chapter Thirty

Visiting Center at the Vandenberg County Jail

"Just looking at the evidence, you're fucked. In fact, even with the illegal search of your stomach, you're still pretty much fucked."

I didn't respond. I just sat there with my elbows resting on the table and my forehead nested in my palms.

"C'mon, Roy, talk to me."

"I got nuthin' to say."

Chick got up and paced around the room for a bit. Then he leaned over the table and pulled my hands away from my head.

"Cop to cop... did you do it?"

"I can't produce any evidence says I didn't."

He sat down again. "Maybe you could tell me what you *think* happened? We'll start from there and try to make a case around that."

"Whose side are you on? I thought you guys were supposed to be working for the DA."

"You haven't been charged yet. God knows the DA wants to! But I asked him to hold off for a while."

"And he bought that?"

"Yeah. For 72 hours anyway. You gotta man up and fight this!"

"I'm sorry, Chick. I got no fight left. This isn't the first time this has happened to me."

"What *was* the first time?"

"Back when I was in CID. I was getting close to a serial murderer. He liked to garrote his victims. Always women, always blond. Anyway, I was getting close, so he sends me a letter telling me to back off, which of course I didn't. So I come home one day and find my wife and child garroted in the bedroom. All her hair was cut off. They pulled me off the case. Said I was no longer objective. Anyway, one day they find this stiff they believed was the killer only I *knew* it wasn't."

"How'd ja know?"

"Hunch maybe. Wait, no. *Way* more than a hunch. I *knew* it. I don't know how I knew it, I just did."

"So then what happened?"

"They closed the case. Eventually they put me back on homicide. But as long as I was in the Army, I kept getting these letters every year on the anniversary of her death. Inside would be some snide little note and a lock of her hair."

"So that's why you wanted to stay away from homicide."

"Yeah."

"I'm sorry, Roy. I didn't know. You think it might be the same guy?"

"Nah, I doubt it. I think the new guy got the idea of taking out Emily and Devil by hacking my emails. I'd asked Emily to dye her hair some other color. The fucker knew I was scared. I think he might have bugged the table we used at Albert's— that's the bar up there. Monica and Sam used to sit and compare notes with me after hours. I told them about my first wife."

"Only by framing you, this guy is doing the first guy one better."

"Looks that way."

"I still need you to help me out."

"Yeah, why's that?"

"Because if you don't you're gonna end up in the gas chamber."

"Chick, the way I feel right now, that would be a blessing."

"Okay, how about because there's still a serial killer out there, and if we don't catch him, he's going to kill again. Putting you in here just takes the heat off him. By the way, that's the argument I used to get you your 72 hours."

I snorted. "I'd like to have been a fly on the wall when you laid that one on him!"

"Think about it. It fits. You have no motive to come down and murder your wife and your German Shepherd. And you were damned effective putting heat on the bastard that did this. What better way to get you off his back than by framing you as a copycat? I mean, you're in jail, right? Not out chasing him."

I had to admit, it made sense.

"Okay. What do you want me to do? I assume you're not going to let me out to pick up his trail again."

"Can't. The DA would have us both in here in adjoining cells. But how do you think he might have done what he did? This is a new MO, right?"

"Yeah, for starters he didn't kill Emily before he went to work on her. Up on the stations, he always killed his victims so they wouldn't put up a fight and attract attention. Emily was still alive when I walked in."

"So what happened after you walked in?"

"He turned my lights out."

"How?"

"Sap, a soft one—lead shot instead of a lead slug. Whacked me above the right ear."

"How do you figure that?"

"Cause I'm sitting here alive telling you about it. Lead slugs are almost always lethal when administered to the skull."

"Why didn't you tell us about getting knocked out?"

"You didn't ask."

"Okay, my bad. What did you see before you got sapped."

"Not much. Emily was hanging from the ceiling, nude, back to me, lot of blood pooling under her. Devil was lying in the corner. Didn't get much of a look at him. That's it."

"Were the lights on?"

"Yeah. Blinds drawn too. Saw that from the street walking in."

"That strike you as odd, given the late hour?"

"No. I'd texted Emily from Edwards. I expected her to be sleeping on the couch waiting for me."

"What time did you text her from Edwards?"

"About midnight."

"And you arrived home 0200?"

"Yeah, pretty close."

"So the killer had two hours to work on her."

"Yeah."

"How do you think he got in?"

"Probably jimmied the back door, then drilled Devil when he came running up to investigate. That was maybe a couple of hours before she got home."

"You think he overpowered her when she walked in?"

"I figure he was waiting behind the front door. She would have spotted Devil lying in the corner all bloody. That's when he would have jumped her."

"How'd he subdue her? There were no reports of screams from the neighbors."

"I figure he came up behind her and slapped duct tape across her mouth. Then he strong-armed her to the floor and sat on her while he injected her with Flunitrazepam, a 'roofy.' I'm guessing it was a low dose—couple of milligrams—so she'd be real woozy and easy to manage. I'm also guessing he wanted her to see herself being 'vampired' by me."

"How'd he pull that off?"

"He's not just an electronic identity thief. No, our boy is a regular shapeshifter. He uses 3D printing to manufacture any face he wants. This time he picked my face. He wanted her to think I was killing her."

Ciccolella reached into his jacket and pulled out a flask, removed the stainless cap, and took a long pull.

"You gonna share that?" I asked. He shoved it over to me and I sniffed it. Yuck, bourbon. Beggars can't be choosy.

"Anyway, he probably sat on her for fifteen or twenty minutes waiting for the drug to take effect. When she was out, he stripped her and suspended her to the ceiling by her feet. Then he bit her in the neck with his fake vampire fangs to get the blood flowing, but he didn't kill her. He only collected maybe half a liter of blood and then put some tape on the wound. That way I'd walk in and immediately go into shock. That's when he jumped me. Only he didn't want to risk me overpowering him—he knows I carry a blade and a sap. So, he wanted me all the way out from the get-go."

"Okay, then what?"

"Then he hits me with a dose of Flunitrazepam, a little bigger dose, maybe three or four milligrams, since I'm bigger than Emily. That way he could count on me staying out for a while."

"You're pretty sure of this Flunitrazepam?"

"I figure he intercepted message traffic between me and Monica up on *Einstein*. I had her checking into date rape drugs when we were still puzzling over cause of death. I suggested Flunitrazepam. Guy's a poet. He's trying to 'hoist me on my own petard,' so to speak."

"Yeah, yeah, I'm seeing that."

"So then he glues another set of his fangs into my mouth, injects their canals with blood, Emily's blood, swishes Emily's blood around in my mouth, and finally intubates me and fills my stomach with the blood he'd saved from before."

Chick took another slug of whiskey. I followed suit.

"So then he props me next to Emily and pulls off the tape on her neck so she'll bleed all over my shirt and pants. Then he wipes down the house and packs up his stuff, but before he leaves he pulls the tape off Emily's mouth and gives us each a shot of Flumazenil. That's the antidote for Flunitrazepam. I figure three milligrams for her and about five for me. You're supposed to drip it in, but at this point, he didn't much care if we died."

"Okay, so you both wake up after he leaves. Then what?"

"While we're waking up, she bleeds out another liter maybe. I figure it was only because she was upside-down that she came to at all. Anyway, she sees me and screams, 'Roy, no!' I couldn't talk very well what with being groggy and those damned fangs in my mouth. Let me have some more of that stuff."

Chick passed me his flask and I continued.

"I wanted to tell her it wasn't me. She starts wiggling in a panic making the last of her blood come out. I couldn't figure out what to do. She desperately needed what blood she had left for her brain, but if I cut her down it would drain back into her body. So, I called 911. Then I called the cops. You know the rest."

"What's he gonna do next?"

"I don't know."

"Guess."

"He's going back to CisLuna."

Visiting Center at the Vandenberg County Jail

"You have three options, Mr. Stone. First, you can plead not guilty by reason of insanity. The judge has ordered psychiatric evaluation—routine in cases such as this one.

"Second, you can plead not guilty in which case we go to trial. The prosecutor has a pretty solid case—I'd say unbeatable. He's got you at the crime scene at the time of your wife's death. He's got a silenced 9mm automatic pistol that just happens to be from the evidence locker from a case you worked a year ago. He's got your prints on the weapon and powder residue from the weapon on your hands. He's got your wife's blood—"

"Spare me. I was there. I don't need to go through it again."

"Very well, but I can't beat this case if it goes to trial, Mr. Stone. You will most likely get the death penalty, although it wouldn't be carried out for decades while the appellate process runs its course.

"Third, take the prosecutor's plea deal. You plead guilty in return for life without parole."

"There's a fourth option."

"What's that, Mr. Stone?"

"I plead guilty, no plea deals, no appeals. In return I get expedited death sentence."

"The appeals are mandatory, Mr. Stone. And as far as I know there is no such thing as an 'expedited death penalty.'"

"There is now."

"Well, I'd have to discuss your offer with the District Attorney. Uh... how expedited are you talking about?"

"Well, I'd have to check my calendar, but I think I can fit you in on Friday."

Courtroom

"How do you plea, Mr. Stone?"

"On the conditions that you waive the insanity evaluation, that the sentence is death, and that it is carried out within the week, I plead guilty, your Honor."

"You are not permitted to negotiate with the court, Mr. Stone."

"Then I guess I'm not negotiating."

The bailiff approached the judge and whispered in his ear.

The judge looked angry, glared at me, then said, "I've been called to chambers. Lawyers with me."

The bailiff said, "All rise!"

Thirty minutes later the judge returned to the courtroom.

"Very well, Mr. Stone. After consulting my law books, it seems that recent Sierra law does allow for expedited executions under special circumstances. Your request is granted. Execution by gas chamber will be Friday morning at 6 a.m. at San Quentin Prison. May God have mercy on your soul."

The Gas Chamber Area at San Quentin

My execution at San Quentin was nothing if not sensational. Executions in Sierra's San Quentin prison used to be carried out by lethal injection. Then when the great state of

Oklahoma screwed up the procedure, that method was abandoned and they went back to using the gas chamber.

Sodium thiopental is used during lethal injection executions to numb the pain of the potassium chloride that stops the heart. It seems that when the drug supplier that provided Oklahoma with sodium thiopental decided to cut them off, Oklahoma prison officials decided to experiment with a mixture of midazolam, vecuronium bromide, and potassium chloride. Their first test subject was an unfortunate fellow named Clayton Lockett. He took 43 minutes to die all to the accompaniment of much groaning, writhing, and convulsing. Pretty gruesome. Lockett was no Boy Scout, mind you. He was in the process of burying one of his victims alive, a young woman named Stephanie Neiman, when at the last minute he fired two shotgun blasts into her. Still, you'd think that the nation that invented television could come up with a way to instantly and painlessly snuff out someone's life.

Anyway, it was largely because of those fine prison officials in Oklahoma back in April 2014 that I found myself looking into the hatchway of San Quentin's gas chamber on this Friday morning in April 2075. There was now a single chair where there used to be two. It's made of metal mesh— no padding—and has straps for your arms, chest, and legs. The interior color of the chamber—and it is indeed a chamber—is kind of what can only be described as government bureaucrat green. Beyond the chair are a panel of six windows. Beyond the windows are partitions, I gather to separate the friends of the bride from the friends of the groom, and also the prison officials. The only thing missing was a concession stand for soft drinks and popcorn.

Once they get you strapped in, the chair pivots around so you can face your audience. At this point one of the guards places a clear plastic mask over your mouth and nose and straps it in place. The strapping part was pretty vigorous— apparently some dumb schmuck tried to shrug it off in mid execution by rubbing his face against his shoulder. Then the guard hooked up a pair of leads to a heart monitor strap that was secured around my chest.

When all was done the guard smiled, patted my shoulder, and asked, "Are you comfortable?"

I gave him an exasperated look. My freaking heart was running like a snare drum riff and my breathing was doing a pretty good job keeping pace.

Then the guard leaned down and whispered, "Don't worry. You won't feel a thing. It will be just like going to sleep!"

Huh! Says he. Then he stepped outside and I heard the hatch being dogged shut behind me.

Alone inside the chamber, I heard the warden's voice over the loud speaker. "Can you hear me?"

I nodded. "I'm throwing the gas switch now. Please start a slow count backwards from ten."

I looked at him funny, blinking in the barrage of flash bulbs going off.

"Out loud, please. We need to know how you're doing."

I guess I imagined my death scene would be more Shakespearean. In reality, it was more Kafkaesque.

I started counting. I think I maybe got to seven.

Chapter Thirty-One

The headline was straight out of the pulps, "Killer Cop Gets Gas." There was a ghoulish video of me in my 'death throes.' Pretty cool. My face was recognizable in spite of the plastic mask—that was important. Still more important was that I looked dead when it was over. And I did, including pissing myself—you could see that dripping from my crotch in the vid. Nice touch.

We were on *SLS John Marmie*, named for the deputy project manager of the LCROSS, or Lunar Crater Observation and Sensing Satellite, a NASA mission from way back in 2009, according to the plaque on the bulkhead. I was an expert space passenger now, so I got up and floated around after we entered the cruise phase of the trip. Marmie's color portrait was next to the plaque. Dapper fellow. Wore a necktie that gave him a real retro look. And to think my leather flight jacket was considered a throwback. Anyway, LCROSS found water at the lunar polar caps. I guess that was a big deal back then. You'd think that much water would have been obvious.

We were in a race to beat the killer back to *Borucki*, and *Marmie*, being a LEO shuttle, was our best shot. I *knew* *Borucki* was where that bastard was headed, but what it boiled down to was still just a hunch.

"So how did I die?" I asked Ciccolella.

"Admirably. An example for us all."

"No, I mean how did you 'kill' me?"

"Oh, that. We used a general anesthesia... sevoflurane or something. The mask was hooked up to a standard anesthesia machine. Had to drill a hole through the wall of the gas chamber to bring the tubing in. Warden was really pissed about that. You should send him a sympathy card when you get back."

"Yeah, sure. I'll have to find something in bureaucrat green."

I killed the rest of the commute time by catching up on the news on my communicator. SpaceCorp had given me a new model that was quantum encrypted. '100% uncrackable!' they said. Yeah, right. I still gave myself an alias and made sure that I kept my message traffic as limited as possible.

Ciccolella, Larson, and I had hatched this evil plan that would snare our killer if I was right that he was heading back up to CisLuna. Once we had it down—about an afternoon's worth of work—we sent the details to Rogers, Sam, and Monica via encrypted MLS, or modulated laser signal. That technology was '100% uncrackable' as well, provided the message clerk on the other end was competent and did not forward the contents via regular mail.

We even had a deception plan to go with the real one. We guessed that the killer might assume we were headed up here to catch him. We hoped he would not be wise to our redirecting all the incoming flights to *Borucki*. We also hoped he would buy Ciccolella's press conference announcement that he was lofting a whole army of cops to do a 'room-to-room' search of the stations, and that he would also buy that the search would logically start at the next in line from his last kill—that would be *SSS David Koch*, named for a project scientist on the Kepler mission. *Koch* was a research vessel that served as a platform for a giant telescope to analyze the Alpha Centauri triple star system.

So, we had Ciccolella plus the captain and security chief of *Koch* exchange a bunch of dummy messages about how they were going to fly a huge team up to *Koch* with the advance crew arriving by month's end. We had them use a pseudo encryption that would look like what you'd expect from amateurs. A problem evil geniuses often have is that they think everyone else is stupid. They are correct in that assumption, but their downfall was that everyone else is not as stupid as they think. The key to all successful deception plans is to start with what the mark expects and then build on that expectation.

The real plan, not the deception, was simple. All CisLuna traffic starting from two days before my execution was held up, not indefinitely, just enough so we could guarantee beating him there using a LEO shuttle—a six-hour flight from takeoff at Earth's surface to docking at *Borucki*. The usual transit time was about three days, sometimes five what with transfers needed to go from Earth to LEO, then LEO to *Borucki*, and finally from *Borucki* to whatever station you were bound for, be it one of the CisLuna stations or the Lunar Surface Stations. For added safety we rerouted all CisLuna traffic through *Borucki*, even if they were ultimately scheduled to dock with one of the other stations. We kept that part secret. Passengers didn't get to find that out until they got off their shuttles. Then we'd feed them some bullshit story about technical difficulties at their planned rendezvous station. Chick's fictional army of cops would play into this traffic disruption ruse.

While the incoming passengers were our captive audience in the passenger lounge, we planned to identify each of them with DNA scans. That was the only thing we had to go on in terms of a positive ID of the killer—that blood sample I got when I knifed him coming out of my room. Everything else about the perp was an unknown. His physical appearance changed whenever he felt like it using 3D printer technology. He never left prints at the crime scene, so there is no way to ID him from prints. He changed his electronic signature at will. Sometimes we'd catch him in a duplication—the same two people don't usually eat at the same time in different cafeterias. But those minor *faux pas* never lasted long enough to do us any good.

Assuming we ID'd the killer in the passenger area, and assuming he had not managed to smuggle in some kind of laser zap gun in his duffel bag, and assuming Rogers' goons were quick enough and gooney enough, and assuming—ah, fuck it. This was starting to feel like more of a crap shoot than a plan.

I felt the familiar shapes of my blade and sap underneath my space suit. SpaceCorp bureaucracy forced us to arrive naked of firearms once again. My original 28-cm blade and thumb sap were still in the evidence locker down at Vandenberg PD. They confiscated them when they arrested me. I was packing spares, a 33-cm spring-assisted blade and a 28-cm 4-ply sap filled with a solid lead slug instead of lead shot.

The spring-assisted blade was something I had been experimenting with. Technically, switchblades are illegal in Sierra. Spring-assisted knives are legal. They open fast enough, but you have to be careful that you hold them right-side up in your hand or your finger would be on the wrong lever. For some reason, I never had that problem with my switchblade—must have been the feel of my thumb on the button. Getting your index finger on the lever is easy enough when you're practicing, but not so easy when it's a real fight. You needed the muscle-memory that came from drawing and opening a knife thousands of times—something I had not had time for while I was getting ready for this mission. Who knew what might come of a longer blade and a longer sap if this case did come down to hand-to-hand combat? Another three cm on my blade when I stabbed him the last time and Emily might still be alive. Part of me hoped it would come down to hand-to-hand.

The flight technician pulled on my space suit sleeve. "Sir, we're on final for *Borucki*. Better check your straps."

Monica had the DNA ID procedures set up in the passenger area as we pulled into the hangar bay. When you take off from Earth in a LEO shuttle you are seated in an upright position. When you dock with the outer rim of a station you are suddenly pulled upward out of your seat by centrifugal force. The landing maneuver is somewhat like landing a toy airplane on a tire that's rolling down a driveway. The airplane has to match velocity with the edge of the tire so that on touchdown the tail, belly, and nose hooks catch the arrestor cables and keep the shuttle from bouncing off into space. It's similar to a carrier landing but more exacting. Apart from Patty's one-time miracle, they've never come up with a manual way to pull it off. Either the computer gets it right or you do a go-around. After docking, your straps hold you in place upside-down. You have to be careful getting out of them or you'll land on your head. A fall could be fatal if you bust a face plate since the hangar bay is evacuated.

You exit a shuttle docked at a station through a hatch in the shuttle belly. A ladder extends up into the passenger area and the passengers descend to the hangar deck. I didn't like it that it was so easy to step out of line once you got to the deck above. You could go scurrying off into the darkness of the hangar bay and nobody would find you.

A LEO shuttle can hold up to thirty passengers but the airlock leading into the passenger area is only big enough for ten, so it can get congested around the outer airlock door. That worried me too. Sneaky people use congestion to disappear.

I decided to check out the hangar area before entering the passenger area to make sure Rogers had a couple of his more muscular men on hand in case the killer smelled a rat while riding in on his shuttle. Two of Rogers' more muscular goons jumped me, wrestled me to the deck, and cuffed my hands behind my back with nano-ties before hustling me into the airlock. Once through the airlock, they pulled my helmet off. Their surprise told me Rogers had followed my other instructions—don't tell anyone I'm still alive unless they absolutely need to know. Then they fucked up.

Monica walked toward me all smiles, "Roy! Welcome back from the dead!"

She was about to give me a big hug when I yelled, "Stop!" My angry tone jerked her up short.

"What's wrong?"

"How do you know I'm Roy Stone?" I pinched at my cheek, "How do you know this is the real me and not some 3D likeness of me glued on for effect?"

Monica looked like somebody whacked her across the face with a dead mackerel.

"Oh, god, he's right! Hold him while I get a swab."

I opened my mouth while she rubbed a cotton swab against the inside of my cheek. She stuck it in her DNA machine and waited a minute.

"He's clean." Then she called Chick and the flight technician over and gave them the same treatment.

Rogers came over, "Sorry, boss."

"That's okay. It was a good lesson. Meanwhile, there's not enough guards in the hangar area. You have two. You need at least eight. There were only three passengers on this flight, not counting the crew. What happens when you have thirty?"

Rogers looked glum.

"Buck up. That's why we drill—so we don't fuck up when it's show time."

I winked and slapped him on the shoulder. "Okay, let's look at contingencies. What happens when you have a crowd of people and they're bunched up at the airlock and somebody starts screaming that they ran out of oxygen?"

"We hook them up to an umbilical."

"*Who* hooks them up? You or a technician?"

"Well, I guess if they're turning blue, whoever's closest."

"Wrong answer. Technicians deal with passenger problems. Guards guard. Do not let yourselves be played for suckers. This guy is scary smart and ruthless as a crocodile. He won't hesitate to bash your faceplate in if he thinks you're on to him." I hesitated to let that sink in.

"Another policy we need to implement is nobody gets to carry their baggage into the passenger terminal with them. It's too easy to hide a pry bar or something worse inside one. This guy will not hesitate to pull out a blade and open up your suit."

"Next question—how do the passengers get their carry-on baggage off the shuttle?"

Nobody answered.

"They don't," I said. "Use the flight technicians as baggage handlers. Just make sure whomever you pick is trustworthy. And make sure *all* the passengers are off the shuttle before you send flight technicians back on to retrieve baggage."

A few nodded. Everybody tried to look cooperative in the aura of my intense paranoia.

"Okay, where are Lijuan and Mak?"

"Right here, boss!"

By then I was out of my outer suit and down to my inner liner. I'd soiled it on the flight and it smelled from urine. "I need to clean myself up a bit. How soon is the next incoming flight?"

"That would be SpaceCorp LEO Shuttle *SLS Butler Hine,* about four hours from now, boss."

Back in the day, Butler Hine was a top project manager on LADEE or Lunar Atmosphere and Dust Environment Explorer, another Tony Colaprete mission that provided us so much of our early knowledge of the rich water resources on the moon.

"Okay, let's meet in the war room in thirty minutes. What have we got on the incoming passengers? I want to cross-reference their pics and names from the passenger manifest with any other databases in SpaceCorp. What we're looking for is a name with mismatched pictures."

The War Room

"Where's Rogers?" I asked.

"He's busy finding more people to guard the passenger and hangar areas," Lijuan said.

"Good, let's get started. What have you got, Mak?"

"Does it have to be a man, boss?" Mak asked.

I thought a moment. "No it does not."

Mak projected a pair of pictures of a woman named Marla Savage. She was an attractive blond in one picture and brunette in the other. Facial features were similar but not identical, like you might expect from ID pics taken five years apart.

"Is it possible this individual just colored her hair?" Lijuan asked. "You know, it's not safe to be a blond up here these days."

Ciccolella asked, "Is it public knowledge that the killer prefers blonds?"

"Not officially," Monica said. "Victims' names have been published and their identities may have been known around the crew. It's possible some folks are putting two and two together."

"Okay, set Ms. Savage aside. Next?"

Mak put up the ID photo of a middle-aged white male named Barnaby Brown.' The first picture was a middle-aged male with a bald head. Nobody recognized the second picture. Except me.

"That's Jonathan Teach aka Simon Crowne."

I watched *Butler Hine's* approach on the big wall monitor inside *Borucki's* Passenger Area. She lacked the graceful lifting surfaces of *John Marmie*. She had no need of them since she would never enter Earth atmosphere. Her sole function was to make a continuous loop between LEO and CisLuna. She used the same hook retention system as *John Marie*—a tail hook, two belly hooks, and a nose hook—but she had 'pogo sticks' in lieu of wheels. They were heavily damped with shock absorbers to cushion the impact and provide stability afterwards. They did not need to slide like wheels because she would never land on a runway.

We intended to apprehend Passenger Barnaby Brown as he waited for his turn at the airlock. All space suits have name tags fastened over the left breast with hook-and-loop tape. Once his wrists were secured behind his back, we would escort him through the airlock and into the terminal where we would remove his helmet and collect his DNA sample.

By now Rogers had eight goons inside the hangar bay— two at the belly hatch, two on the hangar deck, and four checking IDs at the airlock outer hatch. I was observing the airlock outer hatch from a monitor inside the passenger area. That was where we would apprehend Mr. Barnaby Brown aka Jonathan Teach aka Simon Crowne.

As *Butler Hine* descended into the lower hangar bay, it looked funny upside down. The shuttle's belly hatch opened and a ladder extended inside from the deck. A few minutes later passengers began descending the ladder onto the deck pausing to have their nametags checked. About eight passengers went by this way before Brown took his place at the top of the ladder. Two guards looked him over and let him pass to the airlock. It was hoped that would give him a false sense of confidence. He would not know that the guards on the deck sent a heads-up to the guards at the airlock.

At the airlock, two guards on the ID team grabbed him and secured his hands behind his back. Before they escorted him into the airlock, another team moved the passengers already waiting inside back outside the airlock. Based on their arm waving, some of them appeared not to like that, but they became cooperative when they saw Brown with his hands secured. The ID team escorted Brown through the airlock inner hatch and turned him over to another pair of guards not wearing space suits.

I moved closer to Brown. The guards pulled his helmet off and immediately I saw that it was not Teach. Worse it was not Brown. I walked up to him thinking he would betray himself with the shock of seeing me still alive. He did not. Instead he just looked like a guy who was confused at why he was being treated this way.

"Keep him cuffed and get his DNA sample."

Monica stuck a cotton swab in his mouth and then into her machine. A minute later she said, "It's not him."

I walked up and said, "What's your name, sir?"

He looked at me funny but didn't answer.

"What's your fucking name?" I shouted.

That startled him out of his stupor. "Dinsmore. Martin Dinsmore."

I ripped his nametag off his suit. "What does this say?"

Now he looked really confused.

"What does it say?" I shouted.

"Barney Brown."

"Read it again!"

"Barn... Barnaby Brown," he said.

Ciccolella came over saying, "Okay, keep him in his suit with his hands cuffed and stick him in the tank until we sort this out."

Two guards escorted Mr. Brown/Dinsmore out of the passenger area into the holding cell we had rigged up for persons of interest.

The airlock door opened and the next group of passengers came out to begin looking for lockers to stow their suits in. I moved to the far side of the room. As the passengers entered the room, they removed their helmets and gloves. That was when I saw him, Jonathan Teach. I signaled Chick and Rogers by squelching my communicator. They followed my gaze toward Teach and nodded. I was looking forward to pulling that mask off to see who he really was.

Teach looked over at the table where Monica was working. It took less than a second for comprehension to color his expression. I cursed myself for not having Monica's work area partitioned off from the rest of the passenger area.

At that moment Teach turned toward the airlock and attempted to make his way past the guards. I couldn't make out his exact words, but it sounded like he wanted back on the shuttle. Something about ID paperwork in his carryon bag. The guards wouldn't let him through. Teach turned and looked around the passenger area. I hid my face by tilting my hat brim down and lifting my tablet to look like I was reading it. Teach hurried back over to his locker and begin scrambling out of his suit. He was wearing a standard coverall underneath instead of the usual layers of spacesuit undergarments. He had one of those new condom catheters sticking out the fly of his coverall. After running his fingers through his hair, he stoically walked over to the line at Monica's table. His right hand was in the pocket of his coverall.

When it was his turn to be sampled, Monica said, "We're screening for cancer susceptibility. There's been a problem with lunar silicates on the stations." She reached out to grab his cheek with one hand while holding her cotton swab with the other. As she did so, Chick and Rogers moved in behind Teach.

Teach must have heard Chick and Rogers' footsteps, because he whirled to face them. In his right hand was a switchblade which he snapped open. Chick was closest and Teach slashed across his chest opening a nasty wound. I moved to within about five paces pulling my knife off my belt and flipping the blade open with the finger lever. I was deliberately slow because I didn't want to fumble with the blade lever being on the wrong side. But I got it open without screwing up.

Teach must have heard my blade's distinctive click because he spun around to face me.

"You!" he hissed.

His expression looked strangely artificial, wrinkling in ways a normal face would not. It hadn't occurred to me that a 3D-printed face might not duplicate the suppleness of human facial skin.

Rogers moved in to restrain him, but Teach whirled back and slashed Rogers' left shoulder. Rogers backed away fumbling for the night stick at his belt. Teach pursued him, his right arm drawn back to make a thrust for Rodger's midsection. As the blade was thrusting forward, Monica kicked him in the tailbone, then dropped back a half step and got into her fighting crouch. Teach howled from the pain and advanced on her grabbing her front coverall with his left hand, his right hand drawing the knife back for a thrust. The bastard was scary quick.

I still wasn't close enough to reach them, so I threw my blade. It sailed true without flipping, missing Monica's cheek by mere centimeters. It struck Teach squarely in the forehead, burying itself halfway. Teach froze. Then his legs buckled and his body squatted onto his knees. He held that position so long I began to doubt if he was really dead. Then he rocked onto his back with a loud thump, his arms spread-eagled, his right hand refusing to release the switchblade. A stream of crimson ran down the side of his face, haloing his head on the deck tiles.

Rogers ran up and put his foot on Teach's right wrist and used his night stick to skitter Teach's knife across the deck toward me. I stopped it with my shoe and bent to pick it up with my handkerchief. It was my old Latama. The bastard had taken my fucking knife while he had me looped on Flunitrazepam the night he killed Emily.

Even though Teach was obviously dead, Rogers was very tentative as he bent to check for a neck pulse. After some moments of probing around with his fingertips he said, "I think he's dead."

"Cuff him anyway."

Monica ran over to Chick to render first aid. He had a nasty cut and he'd bleed out soon without attention. The slash was deep, cutting his left subclavian artery as it passes over the first rib before it hides under the collar bone. I kept that blade sharp as a scalpel, honing it regularly on a piece of ultra-fine emery cloth and stropping it on my pantleg. Monica put pressure on the wound with her palms and yelled, "Get some corpsmen in here, STAT!"

One of the guards made the call, "We have an officer down. Knife wound to the chest. Extensive bleeding... Yes, we're doing that... Get here fast... It's spurting."

I reached down to retrieve my knife from Teach's forehead.

Ciccolella, ever the cop, yelled, "Leave it!"

I looked at him. "Evidence," he said, grinning.

Rogers asked, "We got our man, boss. Should we let the rest of them through?"

"No, this is a crime scene. Check them all. Nobody leaves the passenger area till their DNA clears. Start with that piece of garbage on the floor."

SLS John Marmie

The headline on the newsfeed this time was not so classic. "Killer Cop Back from Dead." Assholes. Couldn't they at least say I was exonerated?

We had to wait a week before it was safe for Ciccolella to suit up for the ride home. There was a corpsman escorting us but her presence was mostly cosmetic. The shuttle interior was in vacuum and if his wound opened during the flight, there would be little she could do to save him. We had an escort flight technician also—company policy when you're not an astronaut. I didn't mind—there was still a lot I didn't know about flying around in space in spite of my extensive 'tourist' experience.

"So what are you going to do next?" Ciccolella asked.

"I'm not sure. There sure as hell isn't anything left for me on Earth. I'm told Emily and Devil were cremated. They said I can have their ashes if I want them."

"That was a nice touch, Devil and all. They don't usually make so much fuss over pets."

"Yeah, I guess it was."

"I heard Larson wants to talk to you when you get back."

"Yeah, he wants me to convert the security force up here into a real police force. It's a pretty good offer—I'd get to travel around to all the stations. Live out my days in space."

"You know you could take Emily and Devil up to the lunar surface. Put their ashes someplace where you could see them anytime you looked up."

"Yeah? Where would that be?"

"I dunno. Tycho Crater is easy to spot. You can see it with the naked eye. The Helium-3 crew could give you a lift—I hear they're doing some survey work there." He paused to peck away at the keyboard on his computer. His glove tips had little nubbins on the finger tips so he could hit the keys reliably. "Here's a nice view of Tycho. Check out the mountain in the middle."

I scrolled around and zoomed in on the depression at the summit. It had a pretty spectacular boulder that would be easy to see from CisLuna using an ordinary telescope. It could be their headstone.

"Think they'd give me a lift to the summit?"

"They might. You might be the killer-that-got-away-on-a-technicality in the eyes of the press Earthside, but up here you're like Jesus. You died so you could come back and save them."

"Jesus? That's a stretch. Maybe I could be one of the lesser saints. Besides it was a team effort. And we both know the result is at best temporary."

"You take Larson up on his job offer and you could stretch 'temporary' out quite a ways. Decades maybe. Give him a call when we get down."

"Maybe I will."

CHAPTER THIRTY-TWO

Vandenberg

It was a week after returning Earthside before I was able to collect Emily and Devil's cremated remains. It was painful. Predictably, I felt like it was my fault they were dead. If only I'd had my .357 when I caught him in my room. If only my knife hadn't missed his bowel. If only I'd caught the bastard before he returned to Earth instead of following his false trail to the lunar surface. If I really wanted to beat myself up, and it seems that I did, I could play the if-only game with Patty and Melody as well. It was always a race with serials. Stop them before they kill again. A race where you're trading bodies for clues. A race where the more you gain on the perp, the greater the odds he will circle back and bushwhack you.

I decided Tycho Crater would be Emily and Devil's final resting place. The logistics of getting them interred up there would be good for me. Booze was too easy to come by Earthside and there was nobody down here to keep tabs on your consumption. Joe was good that way up at Albert's.

Down here on Earth, I could see them anytime the moon was visible, well almost. I would need at least a gibbous moon, and of course and a clear night for Tycho to show up. The crater is pretty distinct down in the lunar southern hemisphere with lots of rays sticking out. Maybe I'd get myself a telescope. If I was lucky, I'd get to place them on top of Tycho's 2-km high central peak right next to the soccer-field-sized boulder. As far as I knew nobody had named it, so I decided I'd call it Devil's Peak. For some reason it sounded better than Emily's Peak. The boulder didn't need a name—you don't name headstones. On the other hand, there were no clouds in CisLuna.

Larson's office was in the head shed on the Base. It was big and he'd filled it up with charts and hardcopy books—Jesus, did that man have books. They must have been worth a fortune! There were long sidebars along the windows where he had placed numerous models of space stations and shuttles of various configurations, plus a coffee service. He also had some interplanetary craft and several nuclear rocket motors in exploded view. There was a sitting area consisting of a couch and a coffee table and a couple of overstuffed chairs. On one end of the coffee table was a thick folder, no labeling, very heavy paper. It had accordion edges and a string to secure the flap. I hadn't seen anything like that since the Army.

"I hope you're here to bring me some good news, Roy."

I took a sip of coffee from the porcelain coffee cup he'd given me, trying not to rattle it when I put it back in its saucer. I'm used to big beefy mugs. Saucers are for sissies.

"Depends," I said.

He raised his eyebrows. "Name it."

"I want to take Emily and Devil's ashes to the moon and put them in Tycho Crater up on top of Devil's Peak."

"You mean the central uplift in the middle of Tycho?"

"Yeah, it doesn't have a name, so I named it." I hesitated, then shrugged. "I'm sentimental."

Hank nodded. "I guess you earned it."

"Earned what? The sentimental, or the I get to take Emily and Devil up there?"

"Uh... all of the above?"

"You didn't ask me what you get in this bargain."

"I didn't know we were bargaining," Hank said, "but okay, what do I get?"

"I'll go up to CisLuna and be your Chief of Police. And I'll do that until I die in the line of duty or rem out or you fire me, whichever comes first."

"Deal."

That was easy. He stuck out his hand and I shook it.

"I'm gonna need some support—a cop, maybe detective sergeant level, on each station and another one on the lunar surface. That'll mean three cops for moon duty cause they can only work for a month at a time. The two that aren't on the surface can manage the policing chores on *Borucki*. We might be able to do that with some of the security types that are already up there. Rogers and his crew all seemed pretty good, just need some training—make that *lots* of training—police procedures, forensics, criminal law. They're going to need to be armed with more than blades and saps—I'm talking real firearms."

Larson laughed. "That's gonna go over like a pregnant pole vaulter."

"Emily would still be alive if I'd had my piece up there."

He quit laughing. "Okay, but I'll want to see strict controls about their usage."

"You'll get it. And I figure we could use Monica's primate lab as a forensics lab from time to time. She'll probably bitch about being overloaded and behind schedule trying to make rad-hard space monkeys. Probably hit you up for more lab techs."

Larson smiled at that. "She's up to monkeys now? Last report I got was she was still doing rats."

"And we need some kind of judicial system. This business of Captain's Mast for every little thing is a bit too Captain Bligh—"

"Bligh?"

"Book I read once. Guy was a real asshole back when navy ship captains had the authority of God. *Hang 'em from the yard arm!*"

Larson chuckled. "That could be a problem up there. A lot of our captains like having the authority of God."

"Don't take my word for it. Ask Sam. Captain King. She was none too enthusiastic when she asked Earthside for guidance about trying a murderer, and they told her to figure it out her own damned self. Including executing the perp if we caught him."

"That was my doing. Think she would have done it?"

"Yeah, I do. She was all set to waste Rodriguez. I think she was frustrated because it was taking so long to catch the real perp. It was kind of a 'do something, even if it's wrong' reaction. And that's not right. A separate law enforcement agency and judicial system are needed to keep station captains respectful of due process. Anyway, I could set all that up."

"You expecting a crime wave?"

"Hope not. Although the last one was a dilly. Look, it's not like you don't have the room up on those stations. And lastly, I want improved IT security. Your network has more holes than a... well, it's not very good. And I'll be the first one to tell you that no IT network is 100% secure—and I don't want to hear about your new quantum computers—but I at least want to make it harder for some evil fiend to compromise us."

Larson sat there arms splayed along the back of the couch and nodding as I spoke. Then he said, "Okay, take care of your wife and dog's remains and then let me know what you need."

I don't think he quite realized the commitment he was making with me being chief of police. Then he changed the subject.

"How do you figure to get your wife and dog's remains up to Devil's Peak, if you don't mind my asking?"

"I was going to bum a ride from one of the helium crews."

"Hmm... that might be a tough climb for them. They just have their lunamogs and that slope might be too steep for them. Besides, it would probably be quicker if we flew you up there with a chopper."

"Chopper?"

"Yeah, they're new. They're not really helicopters, there being no air for rotor blades, but they take off and land vertically and have a mission radius of 250 km. Run on four cold gas rocket motors stuck overhead on a mast—LH2 propellant and a plutonium heat source. They don't spin like rotor blades, but the assembly swivels to give you pitch, roll, and yaw, just like the rotor head on a chopper. They don't have a very big payload—about six EVA-suited crewmen plus spare O2. We mostly use them as ambulances for the helium crews and anybody else who gets lost wandering around up there."

I listened politely—the man had just given me what I wanted most right now. I guess he noticed me keeping my mouth shut and nodding.

"So when do you want to leave?" he asked.

I thought a moment. "I guess I'm ready right now. Just grab Emily and Devil's urns and some clothes."

"And you'll want this."

He shoved the thick envelope that had been lying on his end of the coffee table over to me. It must have been old, being paper and all.

It was heavy as it looked. "What's this?"

"Old files we dug up based on the DNA sample you collected on your perp. It's interesting reading, but I'll need it back before you leave."

He looked at his monitor and swished a few windows around with his finger. "There's a flight leaving for *SSS Nathalie Cabrol* in two days. That enough time to pack a change of socks and underwear?"

"Yeah. Two days. Sounds pretty good."

"*Cabrol* is in LEO. I'll send you the rest of the flight connections this afternoon. You should be back up in Cisluna in less than a week. You can make your own arrangements to get to the moon and take care of your business. Tell anybody that asks it's on my authority."

"Can I use that for about twenty firearms and assorted knives and saps?"

He laughed. "I'll need some time to brief the captains about the new sheriff in town. How about you just take what you need for yourself for now. After you get settled, you can send back a materials list and we'll ship it up."

"Okay."

He stood up and we shook hands. Then I turned and left, the heavy folder under my arm.

EPILOGUE

That night back at the house I treated myself to a steak cooked on the grill in the back yard. Judging by the date on the package, this was the one Emily was going to feed Devil. While it was cooking, I made myself a gin martini on the rocks with a couple of oversized cocktail olives. Funny. I only ever eat one, but I made the martini with two out of habit since Emily liked olives but not martinis.

I opened the file Larson loaned me while I was eating. After I finished my meal, I cleared the dishes off the dining room table and started spreading all the papers and pictures out so I could see them *in toto*. There was a lot of shit and I ended up sticking a bunch of them on the dining room wall with map tacks.

He was born Gaddo Ugolino, 2045. Family from the Sea Cliff district of San Francisco. IQ 160. *No wonder the fuck was always a step ahead of everybody.* Graduated high school in 2057 at the age of twelve. Instead of college, he went into an institution for the criminally insane—seems he and his maiden aunt had a thing going, and he was dissecting her in the basement when his father walked in on him. His father described him as very matter of fact about what he was doing, even going so far as to ask his father to pass him a surgical saw.

The aunt's body was laid out on top of a plastic drop cloth. He'd bottled up all her major organs in formaldehyde. Her blood was in a large clear plastic gasoline can. Cause of death was strangulation with a garrote made of steel wire with two large D-rings on the ends big enough to fit your whole hand in. The evidence was unclear how a twelve-year-old boy could be strong enough to overpower a grown woman. Young Ugolino told the investigators how he did it several times—no two alike.

The name Ugolino struck a chord in my mind, so I checked it out. There was a Count Ugolino of Pisa, Italy in Dante's *Inferno*. Gaddo was the name of one of the Count's sons. Accused of treachery, the Count, his two sons, and two grandsons were locked in the Muda Tower and left to starve. *If your family name was Ugolino, why in holy hell would you name your kid Gaddo?* It's like they were asking him to go nuts.

Anyway, young Gaddo escaped the institution in 2060, age 15, and was not heard from again until he turned up at Vandenberg in 2070 under the alias Austen Miller. Police now believe Miller and Ugolino are the same and that Miller was the name he used while perpetrating the vampire killings that went from 2070 to 2072 in the Vandenberg area. They determined this by matching Ugolino's DNA with samples from the dead Barnaby Brown and the blood sample from Jonathan Teach. All matched. We didn't have a DNA sample from Miller. But Miller was concluded to be one of the aliases used in the similar vampire MO wherein all victims were killed by CO_2 asphyxiation before being suspended from the ceiling and drained of blood. I drew a big evidence map on the wall to show matching DNA and matching MOs.

I finally put the report down and took a long pull on my second martini. There was no information provided in the report as to Ugolino's whereabouts during the period 2060-70 save that he was at large. That meant that he could have been in Missouri. He could have been the serial killer I had been in pursuit of. He could have been the murderer of my wife Hanna and my son Michael. *He could have been.*

What evidence did I have beyond 'he could have been?' There was the garrote he'd used on his aunt. He used a similar garrote on his victims in Missouri, and on my Hanna and Michael. It was not implausible that he would have changed his MO when he came to Vandenberg. In fact, it would have been foolish for him not to change it.

He had taken the four people I loved the most—Hanna and Michael, Emily and Devil. Dogs are people too. But I had taken *him*. I had killed him, my life-taking skills finally proving superior to his. Killed him in hand-to-hand combat, the fates having granted my secret wish. Killed him at close range. Close enough to see the deep wound that I put in his forehead with my own blade cast by my own hand. Close enough to see the life extinguished from his eyes as his blood ran down the side of his face. Close enough to watch that blood form an indelible pool around his head on the deck of *William Borucki*. And every time I passed that spot, I would look for that stain and be warmed by the memory of what I had done. That spot, more than any crater on the moon, would be the true headstone of Emily and Devil. Even if they replaced those tiles, as I was sure they would, I would remember... and remember... and remember.

ACKNOWLEDGEMENTS

Nobody writes alone these days, and I am no exception. I'll start with my wonderful muse, Julie, without whom I'd not be a writer at all. She read the very first draft finding several typos and a few plot holes. She emerged from her ordeal declaring, "It's good!"

And I must also thank Douglas Shrock, as much muse as artist. He crafted the beautiful cover art and layout. How many times have I referred to his work for inspiration? You can see more of his fine work in this book a few pages from now where he has rendered a dramatic cover for *Genesis*, Book III of the Galactican Series, our first manned trip to Mars. That's Amanda Blake on the cover with her red hair matching the Martian surface.

Another reader of the first draft was my excellent friend and fine literary critic, Simon Cowan, from London, England. He declared it 'a gooood read.' I cannot emphasize enough how important it is to know if you've got something worthwhile in the early phases after completing your first draft. If first draft readers come away yawning, your best recourse is to trash it and start over on something else. His praise gave me courage to go on. And his excellent suggestions told me how to go on.

Armed with Julie and Simon's comments and advice, I pressed on to the Second Draft, sending review copies out to

Randall Shaw of Kennesaw, Georgia, Trice Healy of La Quinta, California, Claudia Johnson of Portland, Oregon, Beau Riedel of Belmont, California, my stepson Stephen Pinto from Cupertino, California, and my Aunt Ellen Carter from Nineveh, Indiana.

I got good responses from all and am deeply grateful. However, I needed somebody to read the mss who was not afraid (dare I say eager?) to give me both barrels. My good friend Chet Nagle of Alexandria, Virginia was more that equal to that task. I've edited and published three of his fine thrillers: *The Woolsorters' Plague, Iran Covenant,* and *Lazarus Man,* so now it was payback time! He sent my mss back dripping with red plus three more pages of his expert advice. I am deeply thankful for all the time he took and *CisLuna* is a much better book for it.

Next, I would like to express my gratitude to another class of folks who, while they have not lent me their criticism, they have lent me the use of their names for my space stations, shuttles, and the lunar surface colony. There is a famous quote in the space exploration business:

> *If I have seen further than others, it is by standing upon the shoulders of giants.*
>
> **Isaac Newton**

Newton's quote remains a popular sentiment among principal investigators to this day—their way of paying homage to the likes of Johannes Kepler, Tycho Brahe, and Galileo Galilei. The principal investigators and project managers of today will serve as the giants of tomorrow, enabling a new generation of PIs and PMs to achieve even greater discoveries about the Universe we live in.

Since hard SciFi may be described as a history of the future, I decided to give a shout out to my friends and colleagues around NASA Ames Research Center at Moffett Field, California and the SETI institute at Mountain View, California. They have done and continue to do the noble work of science and engineering that goes largely unacknowledged in the public conversation. Let me start with the two fellows on the cover of *CisLuna*, William Borucki and John Marmie. I adopted the arbitrary convention of naming space stations after scientists and space shuttles after project managers.

Bill Borucki is the father of the Kepler mission. He first conceived of Kepler in 1984 as a space telescope that could detect earth-sized planets and determine the frequency of Earth-sized planets in the habitable zones of Sun-like stars. It did not launch until 2009, 25 years later, a testament to Bill's stubbornness or his courage or perhaps both. Kepler changed planetary science. Before it launched we thought our own Solar System was the template for most stellar systems around the galaxy. In finding over 5000 candidate exoplanets (over 2400 confirmed), Kepler and its follow-on K2 mission have taught us that our solar system is anything but typical. Bill Borucki is to exoplanets as James Hubble was to Galaxies.

John Marmie was the deputy project manager of the LCROSS (Lunar Crater Observation and Sensing Satellite) mission. The Moon will figure prominently in future space exploration, largely because of LCROSS' confirmation of large deposits of water in the northern and southern polar craters which, because of the moon's 1.5° axial tilt, remain permanently shaded from the sun. Water can be broken down into its constituent elements oxygen and hydrogen. Liquid hydrogen (LH2) is extremely important as a propellant in nuclear thermal rockets. We could haul it up from the Earth's surface to the Earth-Moon Lagrange Point 1, but that would cost 13 km/s in Delta V. Or we could haul it up from the lunar surface for only 3 km/s in Delta V. You do the math.

Nathalie Cabrol is a Senior Research Scientist and Director of the Carl Sagan Center at SETI (Search for Extraterrestrial Intelligence) in Mountain View, California. She is a planetary scientist, an explorer, and a leader of research projects in astrobiology and extreme terrestrial environments, planetary missions, and robotics. She is a science team member of the NASA Mars Exploration Rover mission and was the main advocate for the selection of Gusev crater as the landing site for the Spirit rover on Mars.

Anthony Colaprete is NASA Ames Research Center's 'Mr. Moon.' He has been principal investigator of both the Lunar Crater Observing and Sensing Satellite (LCROSS) mission and the Lunar Atmosphere and Dust Environment Explorer (LADEE) mission. LCROSS confirmed the presence of

copious amounts of water ice trapped in the permanently shaded craters of the lunar polar regions. It did so by shepherding a Centaur upper stage to a crash landing into one of the southern craters. Instruments on the LCROSS spacecraft would directly observe the ejecta plume from the crash for about four minutes before it too crashed into the lunar surface. A companion mission, the Lunar Reconnaissance Orbiter (LRO) would then fly through the ejecta plume to further characterize its constituents. LADEE orbited the moon about its equator to study the composition of its exosphere and its dust before it too crashed into the lunar surface on the far side of the moon.

David Koch was the Deputy Principal Investigator of the Kepler mission. Noted for his work in spacecraft instrumentation, David developed the  Kepler Technology Demonstration that showed the transit method could detect Earth-size planets. Regrettably, David passed away in 2012—he will be missed.

Butler Hine was project manager of the LADEE mission and also of the development of LADEE's Modular Common Spacecraft Bus (MCSB). MCSB is a low-cost interplanetary bus developed at NASA Ames Research Center. Spacecraft such as the MCSB are essential to NASA transitioning away from expensive custom-built spececraft into less expensive multi-use designs that can be produced on an assembly line at far less cost. The MCSB can be equipped as a lander or an  orbiter on missions to near earth objects, the Moon, and Mars.

This acknowledgement is not exhaustive, limited only to the ones who happened to show up in this story. There are other project managers and scientists around town who have allowed me to name various SpaceCorp equipment and infrastructure after them, including Dan Andrews, Carol Stoker, Brian Glass, Victor Parro, Alfonso Davila, Pascal Lee, and Jill Tarter. They will be featured in future editions of *The Galactican Series*. These folks are my heroes, the genuine articles of space exploration.

I am a patron of Winchell Chung's website. Any writer of hard SciFi who is not a student of this site has rocks in his head. http://www.projectrho.com/public_html/rocket/

COMING IN 2018

In Book III, SpaceCorp has completed construction of SpaceCorp Interplanetary Spaceship *(SIS) Pascal Lee* for man's first trip to Mars. She's not pretty, but with a total Delta V budget of 211 km/sec she can get you there. Her nuclear thermal rockets will allow her to make the full round trip to Mars in 64 days with 12 days loiter time.

Half the crew consists of 100 humans, plus a contingent of six *Pan astra* 'stellar chimps,' genetically altered to resist interplanetary radiation. The other half consists of AIs, led by ISAAK, the ship's main computer avatar. She will carry four landers, two crewed by women, two by AIs. No men, you ask? Fifty years ago, the citizens of SpaceCorp would have raised a similar eyebrow. In 2100 nobody noticed, a testament to SpaceCorp's sociocultural evolution. The greater issue for the crew is whether the AIs will outperform their human counterparts.

Spoiler: *Pascal Lee* <u>will</u> discover microbial life on Mars. Billions of years ago, life on Earth had a chemical, non-biological origin. It was our genesis event. Finding proof of a second, distinct genesis event on another planet is the holy grail of astrobiology. The question is which genesis event produced the better survivors when the two life forms finally meet?

PROLOGUE

November 2101
SSS Jill Tarter, EML1, CisLuna

She opened the encryption app on her communicator and felt the hair rise on the back of her neck. She had composed her message off-line, then sent it in burst-mode to prevent snooping keyboard monitors from capturing her text. Pain in the ass. Even with the communication lag of less than a second it still took two hours to exchange information that could be shared in twenty minutes in a face to face conversation. *Still, what do you expect when you're 320,000 km from Earth and your business partner is who knows where on Earth?*

Partner. Something about that word implied far too much trust than she felt at the moment. They'd initiated the conversation, what, six months ago? She'd ignored it for a week. Comm security on the stations was lax and every now and then you would open your mail to some scam from Earthside. That's all it was. Some stupid real estate scam.

Villas high up on the cliffs of the Amalfi Coast of Italy? How was she supposed to get there from CisLuna? Still, the beautiful images of tiled verandas with chaise lounges arranged under grape vines to look out over the Mediterranean. Where had America gone so wrong?

The prices were ridiculous of course. Especially for someone living on a space station in CisLuna. Nobody got a salary in SpaceCorp's 'work-for-food' economy. Three hots and a cot, plus all the blue fitted coveralls you could stuff into your closet. And recycled air. Suck in all you want. Who cares if a hundred people had breathed before you? And state of the art space suits, especially for the Mars crews. Guaranteed to protect landing crews from cold, vacuum, wind-blown perchlorates, and other crap expected from the martian regolith. Bulky, heavy, cumbersome. Not stylish. Not designed to let balmy ocean breezes waft through the fibers tickling your skin underneath. *Tickling your skin... Oh, yeah!*

She was twenty-seven, born 2074, one year after The Dissolution of America. It had been ten years since she had last stood on Earth. Ten years since she had felt the wind in her face, blowing through her hair. That was at a beach party at Vandenberg the night before she shipped out to begin her astronaut-scientist apprenticeship. She'd done well. One of eight of a class of seventeen to not wash out. She was in line to be a primary, not a backup. If she didn't screw up, she would become one of the first humans ever to set foot on the surface of Mars. She just had to collect her core sample and return to the *Pascal Lee*. Instant fame.

The next clue was a link to an article about Swiss banks and their Byzantine numbering schemes designed to keep dishonest people dishonest. The part about IBAN number formats was yellow highlighted. A week later she got an account number.

CH93 0076 2011 6238 5295 7

CH was for Switzerland. She remembered that much. The 93 was a check sum. Then some meaningless digits followed by an account number. Whose?

A few days later she got another app. The IBAN was filled in along with an encrypted password followed by a big button with the word SUBMIT in the middle of it. She stared at it for a full minute before she clicked on it. The page that opened had her full name, date of birth, and citizenship. The computer camera studied her face for a moment and decided she was who she was, then presented her with a big button with the word BALANCE in the middle of it. Was there anyone on Earth who could have resisted clicking that button? ...Anyone?

CHAPTER ONE – LAUNCH DAY

12Nov2102
S/S Pascal Lee, **EML2, CisLuna**

The now defunct National Aeronautics and Space administration—what historians currently refer to as NASA—funded its first exobiology project in 1959, one hundred and forty-three years ago. It was a simple instrument designed to detect microbial life in extraterrestrial environments. Somewhere along the way, exobiology renamed itself astrobiology—it sounded better—and became a program. The charter for said program was at NASA's Ames Research Center, Moffett Field, California. It was probably no accident that the Search for Extra Terrestrial Intelligence or SETI institute headquartered itself a short distance away in Mountain View. Their charter was to search for any kind of alien life that had a high enough IQ to invent the television or some other device that could send a detectable signal through its atmosphere and into deep space. From insentient microbes to a sentient exosociety, the two organizations had bookended the spectrum of life.

Both organizations survived and to some extent thrived on the belief that life was not limited to Earth alone. They lived by scant data and soft inference. Everything they thought they knew about life not of Earth was based on analogs about life on Earth. If life on Earth needed liquid water, then life not of Earth must need water as well, and a great hunt was launched to find stellar systems that harbored Earthlike planets within their so-called habitable zones where liquid water could exist. If life on Earth was based on DNA, then life not of Earth must also be based on DNA. Lifeforms similar to DNA, say, with different nucleotides, were only fleetingly covered in the literature. And lifeforms not based on DNA at all were relegated to science fantasy film and literature. Even in those mediums, the really far out lifeforms always ended up looking like sea anemones. The less far out resembled humanoids with various sea creature accoutrements, e.g., tentacles, fins, and gills. Hollywood, later Bollywood, was not nearly as imaginative as it thought it was. Anyway, the astrobiology community remained faithful to this belief structure well into the 21st Century when the Age of Ignorance led to the Great Dissolution of the once great nation of America in 2073.

Fortunately, fifty years prior to that in 2023, SpaceCorp bought the rights to NASA's and the Air Forces' space exploration infrastructure. They got SETI for free since it consisted mainly of a community of brilliant scientists who had survived up to then on government grants—SETI was essentially a brain trust with no significant infrastructure to speak of. With no more grants, SETI's scientists moved out of their rented offices on North Bernardo Avenue across the freeway onto the Ames campus, happily subsumed by SpaceCorp's work-for-food economy where living accommodations and other necessities were provided in exchange for research.

While all this was going on, space travel was pretty much limited to Low Earth Orbit or LEO where SpaceCorp was occupied with the challenge of maintaining satellite services in the midst of growing clouds of high velocity space junk. They succeeded, not by providing more satellites, but by moving the satellite's instruments onto heavily armored space stations a kilometer in diameter. The first one, *SSS Wernher Von Braun*, was completed in 2038 after eight years of effort and a cost of forty-five astronauts killed and some 427 wounded by debris strikes. Despite the cost, it was a huge economic success, given that the world had had to go without satellite services since 2028 when Lloyds of London declared it could no longer insure commercial satellites in LEO.

Still the dream of space travel and eventually becoming a true spacefaring society refused to die. Indeed, it was the spiritual glue that held SpaceCorp together—the belief that one day mankind would reach the outer planets and from there press on to the stars beyond.

Today, one hundred eighty-five years after Edgar Rice Burroughs' failed dream of interplanetary travel, the SpaceCorp Interplanetary Spaceship *SIS Pascal Lee* was about to embark for Mars. Her mission, besides the usual flags and footprints, was to search for life. It was hoped that such a find would provide proof of a second genesis, where the first lifeforms originated not from living parents, but from non-living chemicals. Presumably, the first genesis, at least from an Earth-centric view, was the one that began with primitive microbes 3.8 billion years ago. Meanwhile, a second genesis had been the holy grail of astrobiologists for over a century. The dogma held that a second genesis, no matter how minute nor how primitive, would prove extraterrestrial intelligence could exist... somewhere. SpaceCorp just had to find it.

If the word 'inelegant' had a picture in the dictionary, *SIS Pascal Lee* would have been it. She was a testament to why afterthought has no place in engineering design. Back in the days of *Pascal Lee's* initial design, c 2074, her nuclear thermal rockets or NTRs were expected to be the standard closed cycle lightbulb design. Nuclear lightbulbs consisted of a quartz chamber, or lightbulb, housed inside a rocket motor. Uranium hexafluoride or hex was stored in a matrix to prevent fission. At startup, the hex was pumped from the matrix into the lightbulb where it underwent fission. Because the hex was never allowed to escape, this type of NTR is closed cycle. Liquid Hydrogen (LH2) propellant was then pumped into the gap between the quartz and the rocket motor wall where it became very hot from the hex, exiting the rocket nozzle at an exhaust gas velocity or Ve of 30 km/sec, far higher than the 4 km/sec maximum of chemical rockets.

In the initial design, *Pascal Lee* stored its LH2 in a hub that was a whopping 700 meters long. The 200-meter long habitation spokes were mounted amidships, spinning about the hub's longitudinal axis at 1.89 rpm for a full gee of artificial gravity.

Pascal Lee had fore and aft NTRs mounted on either end of the hub—no flip-and-burn maneuvers needed to accelerate and decelerate. Plus, the fully redundant complement of engines on either end made for a nice redundancy for a crew embarking on the first mission to Mars. Total elapsed time of the mission was to be 153 days with 13 days in Mars orbit to put landers on the surface, collect core samples, and return them to the mother ship in hopes of finding proof of life buried within.

But in 2085 a minor breakthrough happened. The lightbulb NTRs were augmented with open cycle gas core NTRs that had a Ve of 50 km/second. They were messy contraptions, spewing radioactive uranium hexafluoride or hex out their nozzles along with the usual complement of gamma radiation. Hub length increased to 800 meters, but the mission duration was reduced to only 93 days.

Six years later in 2091, a major breakthrough happened. The open cycle gas core NTRs were tweaked to achieve a Ve of 98 km/sec, but by some quirk of the mathematics of Tsiolkovsky's Rocket Equation, she needed a lot less propellant to get up to speed. Hub length shrank to 150 meters, and the mission duration shrank with it to only 64 days, 12 of them in Mars orbit. The spacecraft form factor now resembled a coffee mug with a pair of thick dowels sticking out the sides. She'd always be the last girl to leave the bar—usually alone—but she was functional. She kept her lightbulbs since they were closed cycle and didn't spew hex all over everything—handy for maneuvering around Mars orbit without contaminating the externally mounted landers. But she still needed robot tugs to maneuver her into launch position at CisLuna's 2nd LaGrange Point, EML2, 65 thousand km above the Moon's far-side surface.

Shorter mission duration meant a lower accrued dose of radiation for the crew. Inside the storm cellar's 3-meter thick nanocellulose walls, accrued radiation would be 0.7 rems for the duration of the mission, and 7.4 rems inside the rest of the spoke where the walls were only a half-meter thick. The exterior of the ship would get an 11.5 rem accrued dose.

Of course, this assumed the absence of Coronal Mass Ejections or CMEs from the Sun, but even then, calculations showed anyone inside the storm shelter would be safe. This would not be the case for anyone trying to wait out a CME on the surface of Mars, but the plan was that CisLuna would provide enough advance warning to retrieve those crews before the CME hit... if they hustled. An average CME could travel past Earth to Mars in about two days, a fast one in less than a day. Without shielding, CMEs could carry an acute dose of over 200 rems in two days. 200 to 350 rems (2-3.5 Sieverts) would result in a lethality rate of 5-50% depending on the quality and immediacy of medical treatment. During the 11-year solar cycle, CMEs erupted from the Sun about 3 per day during Solar Max, and about once per five days during Solar Min. 2102 had been selected for the mission because it coincided with the Solar Min. Nevertheless, the Mars lander crews on this mission were facing a considerable risk and they knew it.

As the countdown progressed and the tugs released their grip, there was no flurry of activity for the crew to buckle themselves into special chairs for hard gee acceleration. At a scant 1% gee of acceleration, lighting the NTRs was pretty much a non-event. Everyone crowded around monitors hoping to see the Moon shrink in the distance. After about twenty minutes most of them gave up and went back to work. It would be a four-and-a-half-day burn getting up to 40 km/sec cruise speed. She'd hold that velocity for about 18 days, then light the forward NTRs for a 3-day deceleration burn prior to Mars Orbit Insertion or MOI. She would burn 24 million kg of LH2 for the acceleration, but being lighter, she would only need 17 million kg of LH2 for the deceleration and MOI.

The Pascal Lee's four landers were mounted to the trailing edges of the habitation spokes. They were called Mars Descent/Ascent Vehicles or MDAVs. Two of them were manned and the other two fully autonomous. They were named after prominent scientists in the past who had pioneered instrumentation for the robotic search for life on Mars.

MDAV-1 was named for Victor Parro García, inventor of the first immunoassay instrument suitable for space and capable of identifying the giant organic molecules common to DNA-based life. This is no mean task given they are likely to be found in a sample containing thousands of different molecules. MDAV-1 would be crewed by Robin Whittaker and Amanda Blake and land at the *Noctis* landing site about 200 km north and slightly west of *Oudemans Crater* at the end of *Valles Marineris*.

MDAV-2, crewed by AIs, was named for Brian Glass, inspiration and lead technologist for the robotic drill used to search beneath the martian regolith for microbial life. An upgraded version of his original design is used on each of the four landers to drill the 30 meters of core sample for return to *SIS Pascal Lee*. MDAV-2 would land in the Northern Polar

Region near the old Phoenix site where vast amounts of water ice were discovered under the regolith in 2008.

MDAV-3 was named for Alfonso Davila, a leading theorist in the Second Genesis concept. MDAV-3 would be crewed by Lisa Weinberg and Shelley Rodriguez and land at *Dao Vallis* in the bottom of Hellas Crater.

MDAV-4, also crewed by AIs, was named after Carol Stoker, a leading scientist on the Phoenix lander mission that discovered copious amounts of water beneath the regolith in the Mars Northern Polar Region. It was the presence of this water that led many to believe that life might still exist on Mars. MDAV-4 would be fully autonomous and land at the base of Olympus Mons.

The reason two of the landers were fully autonomous was that exoplanetary missions beyond Mars might not be feasible for manned landings. Hence, autonomous robotic landers would make the descent, scout around for life, and if found, attempt to characterize it. Hopefully, this life would be DNA-based, making it amenable to sequencing. A sequenced genome could be sent back to the mother ship as pure computer data where it could be reconstructed one physical gene at a time—along with its protein—in a proper hazmat lab. This would be safer for humans on the mother ship as well as preserving planetary protection.

Fully autonomous lander technology was considered an essential strategic technology for SpaceCorp. Truth be told, the human landers were there mainly for flags and footprints. If they made it to the surface and returned in one piece, their mission would be a success. Still, they dragged along a drill rig and some basic instruments on their landers just in case a human presence really was necessary to cope with the challenges Mars might present in guarding its biological secrets.

Each of the landers had the same fundamental mission: land safely, collect 30 meters of core sample, return to *Pascal Lee*. Scientific theory holds that after Mars lost its magnetic field, its atmosphere dissipated in the solar wind and its oceans evaporated with it. If there was life on Mars at that time, it would probably have been microbial, and would have had to take up a new habitat under the regolith away from the damaging UV and cosmic radiation that bathes Mars today.

Most of the time that microbial life would be in a frozen state unable to repair radiation damage that managed to seep through the protective regolith. But Mars experiences regular orbital perturbations that bring warm periods that would thaw out those microbial colonies allowing them to repair their damaged genes and replenish their populations. For these reasons, it is believed that there may yet be microbial life on Mars. If so, and if it is DNA-based, harvesting those genomes could yield genetic riches for the pharmaceutical industry and others. Such a find would make a valuable addition to SpaceCorp's waning satellite services product market.

The Primate House

Roxanne Carvalho hadn't thought of them as animals for over ten years now. They were a new species of hominid, *Pan astra,* or stellar chimps. Stellar chimps were genetically engineered from *Pan troglodyte,* the common chimpanzee, and like their forebears, only slightly different from her own species, *Homo sapiens*. She spoke English to them and they signed back to her in American Sign Language. They would never speak to her as other humans did—a deficiency in the Broca's region of the chimp brain. *A talking chimp! That would have been a trip.*

But they wore clothes, used the bathroom, ate with utensils. They could even get into their space suits by themselves and knew the hazards of venturing out into space without a suit. They knew how to open unlocked hatchways and often did so to wander about the lab when she was working there. They loved cartoons, especially the Roadrunner, and would howl with laughter when the coyote realized he had run off a cliff.

They liked ISAAK, the ship's main computer avatar, with whom they could communicate using ASL. They regarded his image as another cartoon and always expected him to do or say something humorous. ISAAK usually did not disappoint, but neither she nor ISAAK could figure out what the chimps saw in him that was so endlessly funny. She had suggested that he change his appearance to a more realistic, less cartoonish image. ISAAK declined, "They might not recognize me as the old ISAAK."

Roxanne observed the sleeping forms of the six chimps whom she was accompanying on the voyage. Something about their stirrings during slumber aroused her maternal instincts. The primate viewing room was outside the storm shelter that the crew would live in for the duration of the trip. Hence, it was exposed to the same annual dose rate that the chimps would experience. Her visits to the primate house were kept short for this reason. As her mother, Monica Carvalho, had admonished her back at CisLuna, "The chimps are the experiment, not you."

The chimps were the product of fifteen years of intensive genetic engineering to make them bulletproof to the 25-rem per year gamma radiation levels of interplanetary space. In the process, a few other mods had been done. Although their gametes started their genetic journey as true chimps, *Pan troglodytes*, they were now non-violent thanks to some genetic mods from their cousins the bonobos, *Pan paniscus*. Violence would not do on a voyage to the stars. For that matter, *Homo sapiens* would need similar modification in that regard before he would be considered space-ready. Their form factors had also taken on some other features of the bonobos. They were of slighter build. Males were fifteen kg lighter on average than their forebears. They exhibited no obvious sexual dimorphism—males and females were the same size and strength—another improvement believed essential to good order and discipline on a long stellar voyage. Facial features still resembled chimps rather than bonobos, a testament to their baseline genome. Lastly, they were infertile, lacking some essential hormones necessary to procreation. The way these chimps spent all their free time copulating, a starship would have been awash in crew within a few years. Meanwhile, the missing hormones could be injected to allow pregnancy should the need arise.

Modifying them for radiation resistance had been challenging. All DNA is equally susceptible to radiation damage. It's just that some organisms were better than others at repairing said damage. *Deinococcus radiodurans* and *Thermococcus gammatolerans* were able to make radiation damage repairs within 12 to 24 hours after acute doses as high as 500,000 rems of radiation with no loss of viability. 500 rems are enough to kill a human in a couple of weeks.

It was no mean task to insert the necessary genes from a microbe into a complex, warm-blooded animal like a chimp and get them to express properly. Nevertheless, this is what her mother, Monica Carvalho, and her genetics team had accomplished. The chimps were on board *Pascal Lee* as a final proof that the engineering had been effective. A positive conclusion to this experiment would provide the go-ahead for human genetic engineering to begin. In fifty years, SpaceCorp would have a population of space-adapted humans, Homo galacticus, ready to travel to and live out their lives among the stars.

The Bridge

"Well, that was exciting," First Officer Hamilton Briggs said, forcing his voice to sound laconic.

"You were expecting your jowls to be jiggling as you white-knuckled the steering yoke?" Captain Roger Thornton asked.

Ham chuckled, "I grew up watching the old Apollo and Shuttle launch films. I mean, hell, even our own shuttles give you more of a kick when they light their nukes!"

"Goes with climbing out of Earth's gravity well while surrounded by atmo."

"Yeah, I know. But did it have to be so anticlimactic? We're on our way to Mars fer chrissakes! I'll bet half the crew slept through it."

"Cheer up, Ham. Maybe we'll run into a Near Earth Object and you can roust everyone out of the sack to do emergency evac procedures."

Ham's eyebrows raised in anticipation, "Gee, could we? Nice little Apollo... maybe an Amor? Huh?"

"You tell me, Ham. Why don't you check the trajectory plots of all the known Triple-A's now that we have a precise time of departure."

"Aye, aye, Captain! There's only about eight thousand of them, shouldn't take but a second or two to throw a plot up on the holo-screen. I do love this new computer!"

"Nav, you want to plot a trajectory up there for reference?"

"Coming up, Mr. Briggs."

"Okay, Captain," Ham said, "we're twenty-two days to Mars intercept. Nearest misses along the trajectory are shown in red for Amors, blue for Apollos, and green for Atens. Looks like the worst case is an Amor, our old friend 433 Eros, minimum clearance 0.15 AUs."

"Sorry, Ham," the Captain said, "unless we discover a new Triple-A, you're in for a boring transit."

"Hmm..."

"What, no comeback?"

"No, Captain, I was just thinking that if Eros, being five times the mass of the Chicxulub impactor, ever became an Earth crosser, that could be an apocalyptic extinction event— way worse than just wiping out a bunch of dinosaurs."

"Good reason to set up a colony on Mars."

"Want to see another uranium hexafluoride contrail plot, Skipper?"

"Uh, yeah, go ahead."

"Aye, sir, hex plot coming on line. Radiation particles in a nice clearance trajectory away from CisLuna LaGrange Point 1. Looks like the tugs did a good job positioning us for light-up."

"Excellent! Tell you what, why don't you drive for a bit while I go stretch my legs?"

"Cool! Can I honk the horn too?" As the captain walked toward the exit hatch to the Bridge, he signaled the first officer to follow.

"Ham, I know we've done this drill at least a hundred times in the last two years, but now that we're really under way, can you try to pretend like it's a little more serious? You know, good for the kiddies if mom and dad act like adults?"

"Aye, sir."

"That's a good First Officer. Now you may go sit in my chair."

"Aye, sir."

"And don't slouch."

"Aye, sir." As the captain departed the Bridge, the First Officer called out, "Captain off the Bridge!"

The Captain's stateroom was sandwiched in between the Bridge and the Bridge's escape pod prep room. As Captain, he rated a suite—part bedroom with attached head and part office that had a combination desk and meeting table that could seat most of the senior staff. Behind the desk was a full set of monitors that kept him connected with everything important on the ship. The office opened directly onto the Bridge, while the bedroom had a seldom used door that opened into the corridor.

He was known for leadership-by-walking-around and could pop in unexpectedly almost anywhere—the mess area, the engine control room, long range sensors, local area sensors. Sometimes he would even suit up and cross over to the automated spoke where the entire 'staff' consisted of AIs. Ship SOP mandated that all transits between the two spokes required a full space suit.

This walk-about he walked slowly down a corridor that led him by the wing where the landing crew staterooms were. After checking behind him, he opened the hatch and ducked inside pulling up short beside her room.

"Were you seen?" she asked as she pulled him inside. He looked over his shoulder to the upper corner of the room. A CCTV was mounted there, only it had a woman's teddy draped over it obscuring its view.

"You worry too much," he said.

Every room and corridor had a CCTV that ISAAK monitored to locate personnel during emergencies. It was a testament to the realism of his AI sentience that most of the crew felt like they were being stared at rather than just 'located.' Blocking the view of the CCTVs was technically against regulations, but the Captain allowed it in the staterooms—how else could he have a private moment with her?

"Do you have time to...?" she asked.

He shook his head. "Next watch. I'm only supposed to be 'stretching my legs.'" He finger-quoted the last part.

"Did the launch go okay?" she asked.

"Oh yeah. Usual juvenile guff from Hamilton. Had to jerk his chain a little."

"You should have replaced him six months ago."

The Captain shrugged, "He may be a little irreverent, but if things go sideways he's the one I want in the First Officer's chair. Besides the Bridge team is pretty used to it by now."

"I have a drill at the lander dock," she said as she turned and began was stripping out of her coveralls. A pair of nappies and sports bra lay on the bunk.

"What's this one?" he asked.

"Simulated unpacking of core samples and stowing them in the hazmat locker."

"Sounds exciting."

"Only if I fuck up!" She didn't like being stared at by the flight techs while she was in the buff, and they all stared, even the women. For this reason, she had modified her own suit-up procedure so she could put her nappies on under her coveralls while she was still in her stateroom. The nappies and bra were so cheesy they would have embarrassed her grandmother but at least they provided minimal modesty.

By official policy, SpaceCorp was coed. The men didn't seem to mind and adapted to the unspoken etiquette of the shared locker room. Most of the women adapted as well, but there were a few holdouts, usually older women fresh up from Earthside, or the ones that were just too damn sexy to ignore. With her blazing red hair, full lips, and curvy figure, she was in the latter category.

The Captain forced his gaze to meet hers while she changed. They both wore coy smiles, neither fooling the other. She faced him with full frontal nudity. Her thick lips were parted as she looked at him out of the tops of her eyes while lifting one of her breasts with her hand. Then she snickered and marched him toward her door.

"See you next watch, Cowboy!" She stood on tiptoe to nibble his ear while she spoke.

The Captain circled back to the Bridge past the Primate House. He paused by the hatchway that led into Roxanne's lab. He put his hand on the latch, then took it away. As Captain, he could tap into any CCTV on the ship using his communicator. For that matter he could have done his spying back in his office, but he was already here when the thought occurred to him.

Roxanne was in the viewing room, her back to the CCTV. There was too much glare to see through the viewing window. He switched to the CCTV inside the Primate House. The chimps were sacked out in their beds, triple bunks on either side of their sleeping area, the lights dimmed but their images still plain. They slept funny. Some of them shared a bed embracing each other with their long hairy arms. One of them was entwined with his bedding, his hind limb hanging down into the bunk space below.

Beyond them he could make out the apparatus that had been installed for them to play on during the voyage. It had tire swings—made from new tires no less, plus an elaborate network of thick ropes draped about the double high room. It was still a bit cramped by wild standards, but he'd been told it was more spacious than what they'd been raised in on the Einstein. Still, it was six chimps taking up more living space than twenty humans. He snorted.

The one with the hind limb encroaching on his neighbor's bunk got up to use the toilet, his blanket draped over his shoulder as he walked. He wore a T-shirt, but no pants, his oversized balls and penis keeping time with his gait. He didn't knuckle walk the way his cousins in the wild would have. Rather, he walked almost upright, stooped slightly forward to compensate for legs that did not fully extend at the knee. He resembled a little old man with a touch of rheumatism. At the toilet, he followed proper procedures for waste disposal, then went to the sink to rinse his hands. He didn't dry them on the towel that was hanging nearby, just gave them a shake and rubbed his palms on his shirt before returning to his bunk. The Captain raised his eyebrows, then scowled.

He walked away speaking *sotto voce*, "No, Miss Carvalho, you are not going to make a monkey out of me."

ABOUT THE AUTHOR

Mr. Fulsang is an accomplished author with two critically acclaimed speculative fiction novels and a prize-winning short story under his belt. Although he is passionate about good SciFi, he has always felt that he was not space-savvy enough to write a true 'hard' science fiction novel. Not anymore—working as a NASA tech writer from 2007 to 2017 has changed that. He spent that time helping world-class scientists and engineers craft proposals for space missions and getting a unique education in the bargain. The topical areas have included manned Mars missions using nuclear thermal rockets, searching for microbial life under the Martian regolith, extremophiles as analogs for life in high radiation planetary environments, interstellar space travel, asteroids as both hazards and resources, and a good deal of spare time in such arcane fields as quantum entanglement and beamed core antimatter drives. He has become so obsessively conversant in these subjects that he is no longer invited to his friends' parties. Hopefully you will enjoy reading the Galactican Series as much as he enjoyed researching it.

ALSO BY EJNER FULSANG

http://amzn.to/2iNIX4R
2070 AD—The dire prophecies of the Kessler Syndrome have rendered Low Earth Orbit non-viable for conventional satellites. SpaceCorp has solved the problem with giant ring-shaped space stations that protect their payload instruments while housing a large human crew to affect the continuous repairs needed to keep the stations in orbit. But the people of SpaceCorp dream of one day living among the stars. This is the first of the Galactican Series where SpaceCorp moves to LEO. Future books will take them to CisLuna, Mars, the Main Belt Asteroids, the Jovian and Saturnian moons, the Trans Neptunian region, Alpha Centauri, and beyond. New Features in 2nd Edition: --New cover artwork by master space artist Douglas Shrock --New Epilogue describing migration to CisLuna --28-page essay 'On Becoming a Spacefaring Society' --First 3 chapters of Book II, CisLuna.

http://amzn.to/1m9t9XH

FINALIST – 2006 Florida First Coast Writers' Festival

"Sometimes I send some suggested corrections to entrants so the final manuscript is as clean as possible, but your writing is so clean that I would only be quibbling about commas here and there."
—**Howard Denson, Judge, Florida First Coast Writer's Festival**

EDITOR'S PICK – June 2004 Online Writing Workshop for SF/F/H

"There is a lot to like in this short chapter [four], which goes down as smooth as pricy bourbon but still has a wonderful bite."
—**James Patrick Kelly, Hugo Award Winner, *Think Like a Dinosaur***

http://amzn.to/1wmGhcQ

"*A Knavish Piece of Work* will satisfy anyone who studies human nature under fire. From specials on the History Channel to articles in military magazines, we see a special reverence for the fallen comrades. Fulsang's book pays homage to his close friend, Richard Van de Geer, the last man to die in the Vietnam War. In addition, since it's human nature to imagine conversations ten or fifteen years later after the deaths of loved ones, the book conjures up a Twilight Zone twist that takes friends into parallel worlds, where wicked bureaucrats are forced into their special Circles of Hell."
—Howard Denson, Judge, Florida First Coast Writer's Festival

"You have been able to shed a flood of light on a very dark period. You have a knack for telling it like it really is."
—Darryl Kastl, Mayaguez crewmember

Made in the USA
San Bernardino, CA
05 September 2017